breaking free

LOUANN GAEDDERT modeled the hero of *Breaking Free* after the boy she imagines her grandfather to have been. The book is set in Columbia County, New York, which lies between the Hudson River and the Massachusetts border. It is the area where Mrs. Gaeddert and her husband live. Slaves are said to be buried under an alfalfa field not far from their home.

Mrs Gaeddert is the author of twelve other books for young people and of four adult novels.

breaking free

LOUANN GAEDDERT

AN AVON CAMELOT BOOK

VISIT OUR WEBSITE AT
http://AvonBooks.com

AVON BOOKS
A division of
The Hearst Corporation
1350 Avenue of the Americas
New York, New York 10019

Copyright © 1994 by LouAnn Gaeddert
Published by arrangement with Atheneum Books for Young Readers
Library of Congress Catalog Card Number: 93-22600
ISBN: 0-380-72520-7
RL: 4.9

First Avon Camelot Printing: November 1996

CAMELOT TRADEMARK REG. U.S. PAT. OFF. AND IN OTHER COUNTRIES, MARCA REGISTRADA,
HECHO EN U.S.A.

Printed in the U.S.A.

OPM 10 9 8 7 6 5 4 3 2

This book is dedicated to my niece,
Mary Lou Meldrim,

and to the memory of my grandfather,
Richard Bunnell

breaking free

CHAPTER 1

Richard Baldwin had been sad and mad when they had set out from Bennington in the hour before dawn. In the afternoon hours he was still sad and mad—and tired and sore.

He lay across the mare's neck, humming a mournful tune and watching the rocky, puddle-dotted path pass beneath the mare's hooves. Richard's bottom was well padded, yet every slap of the hard saddle sent pain shooting through his body.

His uncle, Lyman Peck, rode ahead, with the reins of his own horse in one hand and the mare's reins in the other. He looked comfortable, as if his saddle were an easy chair. Richard wondered if he had calluses on his bottom, or a pillow stuffed into his trousers.

"Quit that whimpering and sit up, boy," Uncle Lyman called over his shoulder.

Richard was not whimpering; he was singing. The song was "Annie Laurie." He sang it slowly, like a dirge. He tuned his voice low, so that not even the mare could hear him, and finished the last line: "I'd lay me down and die."

1

"Take a look around you, Dick. Trees are beginning to bud. Too bad you couldn't be here for the sugaring. My boys like sugaring better'n anything. Ever been to a sugaring party?"

Richard didn't try to answer the question aloud. He had never tapped maple trees or gathered sap, but he had gone to parties where the sap was boiled into sugar— every year until this year, when Aunt Ruth had been sick. Everything was different—and bleak—in this year, 1800, that marked the beginning of a new century.

Uncle Lyman slowed his horse so that the two were riding side by side. He went on talking in a voice that was nearly a shout. "Should have come with the wagon. Should have known you'd be soft and flabby, Dick. Raised in town and all. Of course your ma babied you, 'cause you was still a baby when she died. Your aunt Ruth babied you, too, not having any other chicks in her nest. Ambrose should've toughened you. His job."

Richard wanted to put his hands over his ears to shut out the roar of his uncle's voice, but he was too tired to lift his arms. He couldn't remember ever having seen Uncle Lyman before yesterday, when he had come to Aunt Ruth's funeral. He had black hair and a droopy black mustache. His eyes were like little brown buttons. Even though the winter was just ending, his skin was dark. He was almost as ugly as the devil himself. Richard decided to call him Uncle Ugly, in his mind. He'd never say those words aloud.

After they had buried Aunt Ruth, Uncle Lyman had come back to their rooms above the store. He had told

Uncle Ambrose that he would be taking Richard to his farm in the hills of New York, just across the border from Massachusetts. "You have no responsibility for the boy," Uncle Lyman had boomed, "no blood ties."

"No blood ties, but he has lived here with us for most of his life." Uncle Ambrose spoke just above a whisper. "He's had no father since he was a baby, except for me, and I have had no son, except Richard. I think of him as my son."

"That may be, but Dick's my own sister's child and would be awarded to me by any court in the land. Farmers need boys and I only have two of my own. We'll be leaving before dawn tomorrow."

Uncle Ambrose hadn't tried to persuade Uncle Lyman to let Richard stay in Bennington. He hadn't said much of anything. Richard pictured him in his mind. Although his body, his hands, his face, and especially his jaws were long and narrow, he looked more like Richard than did the uncle who was his blood relation. Richard and Uncle Ambrose both had pale skin and hair; their eyes were light blue. Uncle Ambrose's voice was soft. Thinking about his pale uncle brought tears to Richard's eyes. He had loved Uncle Ambrose—until yesterday.

When Uncle Lyman had gone back to the inn, Richard had begged Uncle Ambrose to let him stay in Bennington. "I'll never complain about working in the store. I'll quit school and work full-time, if that's what you want. Just let me stay here."

"That's enough," Uncle Ambrose had said in his weak, tired voice. "Lyman has assured me that you will attend a

3

good school. He doesn't have a spinet. That's too bad, but—"

"I'll run away," Richard had threatened.

"I'd be obliged to return you to Lyman. He's your blood uncle; I'm not. You will stay with him until you are grown." Uncle Ambrose had turned away. He was as useless as Uncle Lyman was ugly.

Neither uncle had asked Richard what *he* wanted. If asked, he would have told them that, more than anything, he wanted Aunt Ruth to still be alive. He wanted to live in town, not on a smelly old farm. He wanted to go to the same school he'd always gone to. He wanted to stay near his friends. Uncle Ugly didn't care; neither did Uncle Useless.

The road narrowed and Uncle Lyman urged his horse out in front of Richard's and through yet another stony stream. They rode silently until Uncle Lyman shouted, "Almost home," and tossed the reins back to Richard.

The horses began to gallop. The saddle slapped his bottom so hard that he wanted to screech out, or curse. Instead he leaned farther forward. For a moment he watched the road blur beneath the mare's hooves. Then he closed his eyes and clung to her sweaty neck.

"My land here!" Uncle Lyman shouted proudly. Richard didn't open his eyes to look. "My sheep . . ."

Richard felt the mare make a sharp turn without slowing. When she stopped suddenly, Richard slid sideways. His right foot slipped out of the stirrup and up into the saddle. His head fell down along the mare's body. . . .

He was lying on his back on a packed dirt floor. He

looked at the rafters overhead, sniffed the pungent air, and listened to the sounds of hooves. He was in a barn.

A boy, his freckled face split by a nasty grin, leaned over him. "Fat ain't he, Pa? And white. Hair don't have hardly no color at all. Looks like a plucked goose. Want me to throw water on him?"

Uncle Lyman stepped into view and reached down and grabbed both of Richard's hands. With one swift jerk he was on his feet. Pain shot through every muscle. Black spots clouded his eyes. His knees folded under him.

Uncle Lyman held him upright. "Hurt bad, but over in a hurry. Better than getting up slow."

"Soft, ain't he, Pa? And fat!"

"He's been raised in town. Not enough hard work. We'll toughen him, and slim him down." Uncle Lyman spoke to the boy, then turned to Richard. "Dick, meet your cousin Dan."

"You and me are the same age, Dick, but I'm stronger." Dan made a fist to show off his muscle. His dark hair fell over his freckled forehead. His brown button eyes were like Uncle Lyman's.

"My name is Richard," Richard said.

A tall, skinny young man with a few black hairs on his upper lip entered the barn and began to rub down the horses.

"Zeke, meet your cousin Dick," Uncle Lyman said.

"Name's Richard," Richard whispered.

Zeke turned, nodded, and then went back to his work. He wasn't friendly but at least he didn't bellow.

Uncle Lyman told Dan to show Richard the privy and

then take him into the house. "Tell your ma to give him a bite. Then bed. Hard day. Dick's not used to the saddle."

"What's the matter with that poor boy?" the woman who was his aunt Prudence called as they approached the house. "Is he sick?"

"Just soft," Dan sneered. "Little old ride from Bennington done him in. Pa says to feed him and let him sleep."

Aunt Prudence led Richard into the kitchen. As she dipped thick soup from a black pot hanging in the fireplace, she told him to take a seat at the table. He couldn't take a seat—anywhere.

"Gracious," was all Aunt Prudence said when she saw him trying to bend his knees while he rubbed his backside. She put the bowl of soup on a high chest so that he could eat standing up.

He was hardly aware of his surroundings, except that the kitchen was large and the soup was good.

"My mother, Granny Gates," Aunt Prudence said, nodding toward a little old lady who sat beside the fireplace, knitting.

Without looking in his direction, the old lady said that she was glad to meet him. "Prudence read me Ruth's letters. She said you was a fine lad."

A small Negro child added wood to the fire. Aunt Prudence didn't say who she was.

When Richard's head fell forward, Aunt Prudence took the spoon from his hand and led him to the stairs. He crawled up to a large open loft, supporting his body with his hands as well as his feet.

"We sleep here," Aunt Prudence said, pointing to a doorway through which he could see a fireplace and the foot of a bed. "You'll sleep there." She pointed to a bed set next to the window. "Climb in now and sleep."

"Where are my things?" he whispered, too tired to speak louder.

"Someone will bring them in later. Don't worry. Nothing will be lost."

Still Richard hesitated. Surely Aunt Prudence knew that he needed his nightshirt.

At almost the same moment, she laughed. "You sleep in a nightshirt?"

He nodded.

"Trust Ruth to put on such fancy airs. Or was it that husband of hers? Always thought he was a sissy. So be it. Surely you're wearing drawers under your trousers. Sleep in them tonight. Still enough light you won't need a candle. Chamber pot's over there beside the chimney. Good night, Dick." She paused at the top of the stairs. "I know you're missing your aunt Ruth. Expect it grieved you to leave Ambrose and your friends in Bennington. But you'll like it here. The farm's a pretty place, and healthy." She went on down the stairs.

Richard took off his boots and outer clothes, and climbed into the bed. While searching for a painless position, he wondered where Dan and Zeke slept.

He awoke in a sea of black. The bed was not his own. His arm was touching something soft. He began to sit up and pain ripped through his body and brought memory of yesterday. He was in a bed in Uncle Lyman's loft. He was not alone. The soft something he had touched was a body. He reached across that body to another. The middle body stirred. He and his two cousins were all in the same bed!

From time to time Richard had thought that he'd like to have brothers and sisters. But he had never considered sharing a bed with them. His bed in Bennington was narrow and the alcove that was his bedroom was small and was separated from the kitchen by a curtain instead of a door. But the bed and the alcove were his own. He wished he were there now.

CHAPTER 2

The sun was streaming into the window when Richard awoke alone in the bed. From outside came barnyard sounds. A rooster's crow reminded him of his boastful cousin Dan. From inside he could hear nothing but a few muffled thumps and bumps as someone stirred the fire.

His body was stiff and sore but he *had* to get up. He pulled on his trousers and hobbled downstairs and out to the privy.

When he came back into the sweet-smelling air, he turned to close the privy door. In that instant he heard a whir and a squawk. He felt the brush of stiff feathers against his legs, and a sudden painful jab into his sore backside. He let out a yell and turned to face a huge white goose who squawked again, opened his beak, and rushed forward with wings flapping. Covering his face with his hands, Richard pressed his back into the privy door. The bird flew up and bit his stomach.

"Git, you ole gander, git!" The laughing voice was Dan's.

One more bite through the thick wool on his leg, and

the wings stopped flapping. Richard opened his eyes and peered through his fingers while his cousin prodded the goose with a pitchfork. The goose strolled away, and then turned back to stare at Richard with beady eyes. I'll be waiting for you, he seemed to be saying.

"Where'd he gitcha? In your big belly?" Dan grinned. "Should've told ya he don't like strangers. Here, take the fork with you when you're outside, till he gets used to you."

Richard's hand shook as he reached for the pitchfork.

Dan ran off toward the fields. "Hey Pa, Zeke," he yelled, "gander got Dick so scared he just stood there a shakin' and a quakin' like an old lady with the palsy."

Richard leaned on the pitchfork and looked around him while he tried to suck air into his lungs. Uncle Ugly's farm was ugly. It was surrounded by dark, dense forest; there wasn't another house or a church spire in sight. Uncle Ugly's son Dan was also ugly; so was his goose.

Richard lunged forward with the pitchfork. "Take that, you nasty bird," he shouted, but the goose was walking away and did not turn back.

"Ready for some porridge?" Aunt Prudence asked as he limped into the kitchen. "Then you can take your box and your books upstairs."

"Books? Who said books?" Granny Gates entered the kitchen through a door beside the fireplace. She had one hand on the black child's shoulder. She held her other hand in front of her. Richard hadn't realized the night before that the old lady was blind.

"Good morning, Mother." Aunt Prudence leaned down to kiss her wrinkled cheek. "Dick brought some books with him. Actually, Lyman brought them in his saddlebags." She turned to the girl, who looked even smaller than she had the previous day because her dress was many sizes too big. "Ladle up the porridge, Gee Gee. There's work to be done today. Too much of it." She sighed deeply.

"Me and the boy'll keep out of your way. We'll be reading. I've often thought it'd be nice if Gee Gee could read to me. . . ."

The girl smiled back over her shoulder at Granny Gates. Her skin and eyes were almost as black as ebony. The whites of her eyes and her large teeth were like ivory. She reminded Richard of the keys on the spinet in Aunt Ruth's parlor.

"There's no need for Gee Gee to learn to read. Helping me keeps her busy. You know that, Granny. And today I'll need Dick, too. Another day, when he isn't so stiff, he'll be working in the fields with Lyman and the boys."

Granny sniffed and then ran her hand along the table and sat on the bench at one side. "Sit by me, Dick," she said, patting the bench. "Or would you rather be called Richard?"

"I like to be called Richard."

Gee Gee set bowls of porridge in front of them and put a spoon in Granny's hand.

When he had finished his breakfast, Aunt Prudence set him to work. "Light tasks," she said, "to work the stiffness out of your bones and get you ready for field work."

11

Richard brought wood from the pile outside and stacked it in the box on the hearth. The kitchen was the width of the house, with a window at one end and the stairs to the loft at the other. The outside door was near the stairs and opposite the fireplace wall. On the same wall with the door were two more windows. Granny Gates had entered the kitchen through a door on one side of the fireplace. Richard supposed that she slept in the room beyond.

While he was wondering what was behind the closed door on the other side of the fireplace, Gee Gee picked up a broom and opened the door. She left it open while she swept the parlor hearth. Richard saw that the chairs in that room had padded backs and seats. Flowers were painted on a large chest. Above the chest was a mirror in a pretty frame. Uncle Ugly's house was not a mansion but it was bigger and fancier than many of the houses in Bennington.

Late in the morning Aunt Prudence sent Richard and Gee Gee to the garden plot to pick stones.

"My aunt Ruth's garden grew stones, too," Richard said as they began work. "Where do you think the stones come from? You pick them all out one day and a week later there are more."

"Dunno," Gee Gee said.

"Have you lived here a long time?" Richard asked.

The girl nodded.

"Where are your folks?" Richard carried a large rock to a low spot in the rock wall that surrounded the garden plot.

"Pa's there." She pointed in the direction of the fields. "Ma's gone."

"My mother's dead, too. She died when I was two years old. My aunt Ruth was like a mother to me, but she died last week."

"My ma's not dead. She was sent away. Sold." Gee Gee's black eyes flashed; she picked up a stone and threw it against a tree.

Richard stared at her. "Your mother was sold? Are you a . . . ? You couldn't be a . . ."

"I'm a slave, Master Lyman's slave." She said the word master as if it were a curse word.

Richard had heard about slaves; he had never seen one. Vermont had outlawed slavery when it became a state. The war wasn't just about freedom from the British, it was about freedom to pursue happiness, for everyone, Uncle Ambrose had said. Richard stared at the slave child. He didn't know what to say.

"Hey, you two scarecrows standing there doing nothing, get to work," Aunt Prudence called from the doorway.

Gee Gee went to the far end of the garden and began to gather stones in her apron. Richard picked up large stones and threw them at the wall, pretending that "Master" Uncle Lyman and his rotten son were standing in front of it. Uncle Ambrose had said that owning slaves was a sin. Maybe he didn't believe that. Or maybe he didn't care what happened to Richard, who wasn't his flesh-and-blood nephew. Or maybe he didn't know that Uncle Lyman was a slave owner. He should have asked. Richard and Gee Gee worked silently until they heard the dinner bell.

"So how're you feeling, Dick?" Uncle Lyman ruffled his hair with one hand and slapped his sore backside with the other. "Hear you had a bit of a run-in with our old gander. Nasty creature, ain't he? Dan here should've warned you. It's your business, son, to help your cousin get used to our creatures and our ways." Uncle Lyman clasped his younger son on the shoulder and then took his place at the head of the table.

Richard sat next to the old lady and opposite the two boys; Aunt Prudence sat at the end of the table opposite Uncle Lyman. Gee Gee stood near the fireplace while Uncle Lyman said the prayer. Then she picked up a wooden trencher covered with a cloth and disappeared through the outside door.

"You're frowning, Dick," Uncle Lyman boomed. "Guess you ain't used to slaves."

"We had Negro families in Bennington but they were free, same as anyone else," Richard whispered.

"Well, Gee Gee and Black Boy ain't free but they got it good here. Let me tell you. Food in that trencher's the same as the food on this table. They got their own warm quarters. Good times and bad, we take care of Boy and Gee Gee."

"And Girl? You take care of Girl?" Granny Gates's voice cracked as she spoke.

Richard thought it was good that the old lady couldn't see the scowl on Uncle Lyman's face.

When they had eaten the pork and cabbage and corn

bread, Uncle Lyman turned to Richard. "Brought you a bit of a present to help you over your sadness, Dick."

"Come see." Dan jumped up from the table.

"Pigs is real smart, you know." Zeke spoke in a slow, sleepy voice.

Richard rose halfway from the bench and stared at Uncle Lyman and then at Dan and Zeke. He couldn't believe what he thought he was hearing. A pig? A dirty, noisy, ugly pig? Why would anybody want a pig for anything except to eat?

"Real sociable, most pigs," Aunt Prudence said as she rose from the table and returned with a small wooden cup with milk in it and a rag. "Dan'll show you how to feed him."

Because he couldn't think of anything else to do, Richard followed his cousin to the barn.

"Sows is peculiar creatures." Dan laughed. "Sometimes they just look at one of their babies and decide right then and there that they don't want that one around so they nudge it out of the way. This one is the runt so 'course she didn't like him. She's feedin' the others—there's eight of them—just as nice as you please."

Inside the barn door was a pile of straw. Dan pushed some of the straw aside and pointed. Reluctantly, Richard stood beside his cousin and looked down and gasped. So tiny and white that he looked like a large worm, the piglet was lying still.

"Is he dead?" he asked hopefully.

"Nah. He's just weak. He was born this morning and

he ain't had nothin' to eat." Dan lifted the limp body and held it belly up on one hand while he dipped the rag into the milk with the other hand. When he put the rag under the little snout, the piglet opened his mouth, grabbed the rag, and began to suck. "That's all there is to it." He thrust the piglet at Richard and ran out into the barnyard.

"I won't like you until you're bacon and ham, so drink your milk and grow," Richard said to the piglet. Then he smiled. It seemed impossible that anything this small could ever become a big, fat, dirty pig.

The milk was almost gone when the piglet suddenly fell asleep. Richard placed him in the straw and arranged a light covering of straw over him. He fed him later in the afternoon and again just before supper.

When the three cows had been milked and the hens shut up for the night, the family sat down to supper—cornmeal mush and maple syrup. Gee Gee remained in the background, straining the fresh milk through a cloth.

They were finishing the meal when Granny Gates suddenly banged her spoon down on the table and turned toward Uncle Lyman. "The poor motherless boy brought books with him. You know that Lyman. But you haven't let him have a minute to read to me, me that has worked hard all my life and is blind now and can't do a mortal thing 'cept knit. I want to hear a tale." She patted the table near Richard's plate. "Get a book and start reading, boy."

Richard turned to Uncle Lyman, whose mouth was set in a grim line beneath his droopy mustache. He glared at

Granny, then turned to Richard. "How's your pig?" he asked.

"Greedy. Does he have to be fed during the night, Uncle Lyman?"

"No. But last thing before you go to bed and first thing in the morning, before breakfast. Now I guess you'd better read a page or two or Granny will never give us any peace."

"I could read something from the Bible, or *Pilgrim's Progress*, or maybe you'd like *Robinson Crusoe*. It's exciting."

"What's it about?" Zeke asked.

"A man who was shipwrecked on a desert island."

"Stop talking about what you are going to read and read," Granny cackled.

"Shall it be *Robinson Crusoe*?" Richard asked Uncle Lyman.

"You choose, Dick."

"Wash up and then take your supper to the lean-to," Aunt Prudence said to the girl.

"I'll skip the preface," Richard said. "It just says that the book is worth reading." He began to read.

"Never knew you to take so long washing a few dishes, Gee Gee," Aunt Prudence said when Richard paused to turn a page. "Hurry up there. Boy will be waiting for his supper."

Richard read on. The next time he looked up, he noticed that Gee Gee was standing at the door, a trencher in her hands, listening to the story. The other members of the family were listening, too, even Uncle Lyman.

The candle had burned low when Uncle Lyman slapped his hand down on the table. "Enough now, Dick. Save some for another night."

"That shipwreck really happen?" Zeke asked.

"No. Daniel Defoe made up the story, but he based it on something that *did* happen. Do you like it?"

Zeke nodded. "You read good."

Before Aunt Prudence led her mother to the room off the kitchen, she lit the candle in a pierced tin lantern and handed it and a cup of milk to Richard.

Richard sang a mournful tune while he fed the pig.

CHAPTER
3

It was still gray dark when Dan punched Richard on the shoulder. "You hear Pa call? He says you can't laze around with the ladies no longer. Zeke's already out there milkin'. Get movin' or you won't get no breakfast." Dan was grinning broadly. "You sure had it easy. Bet you never did a full day's work in your life."

"I worked in my uncle's store, all day some days. I stocked the shelves and swept the floor and made deliveries. Sometimes I hoed Aunt Ruth's garden. Sometimes I helped a friend milk his cows. And I went to school. Don't you go to school?"

"No more. I can read and write and figure. What more does a body need to know? Besides, I'm twelve years old, too old to go to school."

"But Uncle Lyman said that I . . ." He had told Uncle Ambrose that there was a good school for Richard to attend. Does he know that I'll be twelve next month? Richard asked himself.

Before breakfast he fed the pig, and then he stopped by the pigpen to look at his pig's mother and brothers and sisters. Each of the little ones—all larger than their brother in the barn—was attached to one of the sow's teats.

"We're pulling stumps, Dick," Uncle Lyman said while they were eating breakfast, "getting a new field ready to plant. You and Dan'll load the sledge with dung and haul it out to the new field." He turned to his son. "Put a pole through the handles so that together you can pull a full load." He turned back to Richard. "We're expecting you to do your share, Dick. Hear me?"

Of course he heard! What made Uncle Lyman think that he might not do his share—whatever the job might be, even loading smelly manure on a sledge—whatever a sledge might be? He didn't know what pulling stumps meant, but he'd learn. He was mad and sad, but he was not stupid or lazy!

He and Dan pulled the sledge, which was a cart on runners instead of on wheels, to the dung heap.

"Don't you have a cart with wheels?" Richard asked.

"Yep. But the wheels'd get stuck in the mud. Ain't you never seen a sledge before?"

"Moves easy," Richard said instead of answering his cousin's question.

The dung heap was foul-smelling, but Dan walked right up and thrust a wide wooden fork into it. He lifted the fork and swung the load of muck into the sledge. Richard wanted to hold his nose. Instead he took a deep breath and held it while he walked quickly to the heap and thrust his wooden fork into it. When he lifted the fork, the muck dribbled through the tines and off the end until the fork was empty. He turned away to take another deep breath and tried again.

"You sure don't know nothin'," Dan sighed. "Hold the fork like this."

The next time Richard lifted a half load. And then he lifted a heavier load. Richard was less stiff and sore than he had been the previous day, but many of his aches returned as he forked the reeking dung. When the sledge was full, he ran back to the barn to fill the end of the pig's rag with milk.

He and Dan pulled the sledge through rocky mud to the field where Zeke was leading an ox harnessed to a stump. The ox strained forward. A tall, broad man, who was almost as black as the night sky, pushed against the stump from the back. As the stump began to tip forward over a log lying against it, the roots were torn from the ground.

"Push harder, Boy," Uncle Lyman shouted.

The big man did not answer or even nod, but more roots were yanked out of the mud. When the stump was free, Uncle Lyman and the man he called Boy lifted it onto a flat sledge. Boy pulled the sledge to the edge of the field, where he and Uncle Lyman unloaded it and pushed it to the end of a row of stumps. The roots tangled with the roots on the next stump.

"Ever seen a root fence, Dick?" Uncle Lyman asked. "Not pretty but it'd take a mighty powerful animal to push through that mass of roots. Besides, it'll last forever."

"Dick don't know how to fork muck!" Dan shouted. "I had to learn him."

"You made good time, boys," Uncle Lyman said mildly. "Now spread it over there where I've plowed. I'll plow it in while you go for another load."

Zeke harnessed the ox to another stump. When the boys returned with a second load, another stump had been pulled. Every time they returned to the barnyard, Richard soaked the runt's rag in milk. There has to be an easier way to feed this little creature, he thought. He also bathed his hands in the stream. The cold water numbed the pain of the blisters that were developing on the palms of his hands. By midafternoon the blisters burned like fire.

"Let me see your hands," Uncle Lyman shouted at Richard, who was pushing against the sledge pole with his wrists.

Silently Richard stepped in front of his uncle and opened his hands.

"Why didn't you tell me, Dick?" Uncle Lyman turned to his son. "Did you know about these blisters, Dan?"

"Soft, ain't he, Pa? I don't have blisters. I have calluses."

"Did you know about these blisters?" Uncle Lyman asked again.

"He didn't say nothin' to me 'bout em."

"Why do you think he was pushing the pole with his wrists?"

Dan shrugged his shoulders and Uncle Lyman turned back to Richard. "Go to the house and show those blisters to your aunt. Tomorrow she'll wrap your hands before you start work. You, Dan, get that sledge emptied and go after another load—by yourself."

* * *

Aunt Prudence clucked as she applied grease to his blisters. He did not tell her that his body hurt as much as his hands. There wasn't anything she could do about his tired, aching muscles. When she was rubbing lard into his hands and binding them with clean cloths, he asked if he could have the pig's milk in a larger container, "smaller on the top than the bottom if you have one."

"Seems like that cup would hold all the milk that a day-old pig is apt to drink," she said, but she handed Richard a tankard with a broken handle.

"Just right, Aunt Prudence. Thank you."

"What do you want it for, Dick?"

Richard was already at the door and he pretended not to hear his aunt's question. He took the pig's rag to the stream and rinsed it. Then he tore it in half lengthwise and tied the two halves together to make a long, narrow strip. Working with bandaged hands was awkward, but he tied a stone in one end of the cloth.

The men had come in from the fields and Richard took the tankard to where Dan and Zeke were each milking a cow. "Can I have milk for the pig?" he asked, handing the tankard to Dan.

"You can have some milk, Dick." Dan turned the cow's teat and squirted Richard squarely on his nose. "Good shot, ain't I?" Dan laughed loudly.

Richard wiped the milk away with the rag. He didn't say anything. Neither did Zeke, who reached for the tankard and filled it.

Richard dropped the rock with the rag tied around it into the tankard and placed the tankard on a flat block close to his pig. He mounded dirt and small stones around the tankard to steady it. When he had dampened the loose end of the rag in the warm milk, he put it in the pig's mouth and sat down to watch the pig suckle.

Someone patted his shoulder. He looked up into Zeke's smiling eyes.

"It's supposed to work like a wick. The cloth will carry the milk out of the tankard to where he can reach it. Think it'll work?" Richard asked.

Zeke nodded. "Might. Your hands hurt bad?"

"Your mother made them feel better," Richard answered truthfully.

After supper Granny demanded more of *Robinson Crusoe* and Richard read for half an hour and then put the book down. He was too sleepy to read on.

"Don't stop," Granny said. "I got to know what happens next."

"Dick has to check his pig," Zeke said slowly as he stood and followed Richard to the door. They surprised Gee Gee, who was standing just outside the door, holding the trencher.

"Boy's waiting for his supper," Zeke whispered.

Gee Gee nodded to Zeke. "Good story," she said to Richard, and then she ran off toward a lean-to at the side of the barn.

Inside the barn, Richard's piglet was sucking the rag. Both boys looked into the tankard.

"The level's lowered about an inch so I guess it's working." Richard smiled with satisfaction and patted the pig as he covered him with hay.

The family was still sitting around the table when the boys returned.

"Dick's made a sow," Zeke announced as he headed up the stairs.

"A sow? What do you mean? Come back Zeke. Explain yourself," Uncle Lyman called to his older son.

"Ask Dick."

Uncle Lyman, Aunt Prudence, and Dan turned to look at Richard.

"How'd you make a sow, boy?" Granny cackled.

While Richard described the rag in the tankard, Uncle Lyman and Dan went to the barn to look at it.

"Just like Zeke says," Uncle Lyman said when he returned. "Dick's made a sow. The runt can get all the milk he wants, and Dick'll only have to fill the tankard once or twice a day. You got a good head, lad." Uncle Lyman patted Richard's shoulder.

CHAPTER

4

The next afternoon winter returned. Snow-filled clouds rolled in over the hills; the air turned bitter cold. By suppertime the ground was white. Richard moved the runt away from the winds into a feeding trough in an unused stall.

Sunday the snow had turned to rain, but the day was too wet and the roads were too muddy for the family to go to church. Richard read the Bible to everyone. He wondered who had done the reading before he had arrived; whoever it had been then, reading was his job now.

While the rain continued, Uncle Lyman and his boys replaced a wheel on a wagon. They mended and sharpened tools. Richard oiled the harnesses, sitting on the floor of the pig's stall and singing while he worked.

Although his body was healing, his heart was still sore.

One morning after breakfast it stopped raining for a bit. Aunt Prudence sent Dan out to kill an old gray-and-white speckled hen. "You go with him, Dick," she said, "to see how we do it."

Out in the barnyard, Richard chased the hen toward Dan, who grabbed her by the legs and swung her, squawking, up from the ground. The hen flapped her wings so hard that her feathers flew.

Dan laughed and swung the hen higher. Then, in one motion, he held the hen against his knee and twisted her head from her body. He threw the bundle of feathers at Richard. The feathers touched his arm.

Shocked and sickened, Richard took a step backward and stared as the hen fell to the ground at his feet. She was dead—she had no head—but she was not quiet. She flapped furiously, rising several inches, flopping back to the ground, moving away from Richard and then back. Richard thought he could hear her squawking but that was impossible; her head was in Dan's hand.

The only sound came from Dan, who was laughing and slapping his thigh. "That's what they mean when they talk about running around like a chicken with its head cut off."

A cat ran across the yard, and Dan threw the chicken's head to her. The cat picked it up and walked sedately toward the barn, the head dangling from her mouth. The hen continued to tumble.

Richard ran to the barn and into the runt's stall, where he dropped down and rested his head on his knees. He hated this place. At first he had disliked the farm because it was not Bennington; the farm people were not the people he knew and loved. Now he despised the farm for a hundred reasons that had nothing to do with Bennington: a nasty goose, a headless chicken, a cruel boy, a stern uncle, a smelly dung heap, blisters, aching muscles, slaves.

A few days later he added mud to his list of things to hate. On the first morning the sky was clear, Uncle Lyman sent Zeke to one field with the oxen to pull the plow and Dan to pick up stones behind it. He took Richard, Boy, and a second plow to another field. Uncle Lyman guided the plow as Boy pulled it through the sticky wet mud, cutting neat straight furrows ready for seed. Richard walked along behind, picking up stones and throwing them into the root fences.

Within minutes his boots were caked with mud so that they were as heavy as the biggest rocks. Just lifting one foot to put it in front of the other was an effort. As he plodded back and forth across the field, his feet became heavier and heavier. The first time he saw a very large rock ahead, he went to it eagerly and scraped the mud from his boots onto the surface of the rock. The rock was too big to throw so he had to carry it to the edge of the field. He set it down and scraped his boots against it again. When he returned to the edge of the furrow behind the plow, his boots were once again heavy with mud. So were Boy's boots and Uncle Lyman's.

Richard kept his head down so that he could not see Boy pulling the plow, the same as the ox was doing in another field. Boy was as silent as the ox and his face was as blank. There was no way to tell what went on in Boy's brain.

It was less disturbing to think about the store in Bennington. Richard had sometimes complained about the weight of bolts of cotton and sacks of sugar. Today they would have seemed like feathers. At last, after what seemed a century, Uncle Lyman looked up at the sky and said it was time for dinner. Instead of going directly to the house, they went through the stream and washed off their boots. Before they went inside they took off their boots. They hung their wool stockings in front of the fire. After dinner they put on dry stockings and their wet boots and went back to the fields.

The afternoon was just like the morning except that Richard's boots felt even heavier and his back hurt every time he leaned over to pick up a stone or a rock. His neck felt ground into his shoulders. He was too tired to try to think of a happier time or to hum a tune, even a mournful one. He just plodded on and on.

And then he wasn't plodding; he was falling . . . falling. . . . He thrust his hands forward to catch himself. His elbows bent and his body and face dropped into sticky, wet, black mud. When he had struggled to his feet, he felt the mud on his face and saw it oozing down his coat and his trousers.

"You clumsy fool!" Uncle Lyman shouted. "Go to the house. Maybe you can be of some use to Prudence. You're certainly no use to me."

Tears were pressing against Richard's eyes, not because he was hurt but because he was shamed. He couldn't open his mouth to say he was sorry; he might bawl if he did. He turned away as a warm tear trickled down his cheek through the cold mud.

"Wash off your boots and take them off and your coat and your pants. Leave them outside. Think you can remember all that? I'll tan your hide if Prudence tells me you've tracked up her house. Hear me?"

Richard nodded and plodded back to the stream. He washed his boots and his hands and face. He hung his muddy clothes on a tree where the wind would dry the mud so that it could be brushed away.

Aunt Prudence sighed and shook her head when she saw him.

"Is it Richard?" Granny Gates called. "Come boy, I need you to hold the yarn so I can roll it into balls. Sit here by the fire."

"After he's put on his trousers," Aunt Prudence said without looking at him again. "What are we going to do with you, Dick?"

She didn't seem to want an answer.

Richard spent the afternoon holding Granny's yarn and answering her questions about Bennington. Did he go to church regular? Did the parson preach good? What did they sell in their store? Did Uncle Ambrose make a lot of money? How many stores were there in Bennington? And on and on. Gee Gee brought them each a cup of tea.

Time passed so quickly that Richard was surprised when he heard the others returning to the barnyard. Uncle Lyman shouted to Richard to come out and help with the milking.

"Oh, Pa," Dan said as soon as Richard entered the barn. "What you want Dick for? He better sit by the fire with the womenfolk. He'll probably pump the cows tail to get milk."

"He knows how to milk. That's the one useful thing he learned in Bennington."

"I 'spect he'll knock over the pail once he gets it full!" Dan shouted.

"Enough," Uncle Lyman said. "He's my dead sister's boy, and I'll do my Christian duty by him."

CHAPTER
5

On his twelfth birthday, Richard carried a load of worry to the breakfast table. Did anyone here remember the day he was born? Had the date been recorded in the family Bible? If twelve was too old for school, he had to make everyone on the farm believe that he was still eleven.

His worry lessened as the morning wore on. His uncle and cousins were too busy dropping seeds into the furrows and covering them with soil to think about anything else. When they returned to the house for dinner, Richard checked on the runt, who still had milk in his tankard and needed nothing except a quick scratch between his ears. Richard stepped through the barn door as a man rode into the farmyard on a big white horse.

"Welcome, neighbor. Just in time for dinner," Uncle Lyman boomed as he rushed toward the man. "Water his horse, Zeke."

The stranger held up his hand. "Not today, Lyman. Wife's expecting me home for dinner. You got a boy named Richard Baldwin here?"

"Sure do. Step up, Dick, and meet our neighbor. Dick's my dead sister's boy."

"Glad to meet you." He handed Richard a package. "Stage brought this down from Bennington for you. They asked me to bring it on out, since I'd be passing this way."

"How come you got a package, Dick?" Dan asked. "It your birthday?"

"Oh, no," Richard lied hastily. "Oh, no, my birthday isn't until next winter, March."

When the neighbor was out of sight down the road, they turned toward the house. Richard set the package down outside the door; no one mentioned it until they were through eating. Then Dan asked where it was.

"Let's see what you got," Uncle Lyman said. "Maybe there's a letter. Wonder how old Ambrose is making out."

Reluctantly Richard brought the paper-wrapped package to the table and untied the string.

"Why doesn't someone tell me what's in it?" Granny whined.

"Because he's still untying the twine," Aunt Prudence answered. "Now he's lifting it out. It looks like a wooden pipe with paper wrapped around it."

Richard removed the paper and ran his finger along the polished wood. Then he lifted it to his lips and blew softly into the mouthpiece. The sound was sweet and mellow. "It's a recorder." The musical instrument gladdened his heart.

"Nice noise, but why didn't Ambrose send books?" Granny asked.

"I'll play you a tune, Granny—when I learn how."

"Not in the house you won't play that thing." Uncle Lyman scowled.

"I'll keep it in the barn, Uncle Lyman."

"So what's in the letter? Read it to us, Dick."

Richard unrolled the letter and held it toward the window away from the people at the table. He scanned it quickly.

Happy birthday, my dear Richard, Richard read to himself. "Dear Richard," he read aloud.

"I wish we could be together" *for your twelfth birthday. I sent to Boston for this pear wood recorder so that you can make music even if you do not have a spinet. You'll enjoy making music of any kind.* "I am keeping busy in the store but our rooms are so lonely at night. Josiah came by to ask about you. I'm enclosing some instructions he wrote down for you so it will be easier for you to learn this new instrument. Here's some blank paper so you can write to me. Your loving uncle" *who misses you sorely.*

"Who's Josiah?" Dan asked.

"My music teacher." Richard dropped the letter into the fire.

"You took music lessons?" Dan asked. "That's sissy. Isn't it sissy, Pa?"

"Seems so to me, son." Uncle Lyman fingered his mustache. Then he rose from the table. "There's work to be done."

Before he went to the field, Richard rewrapped his new recorder and took it to the barn. "This stall will be my music room," he said to the runt. "You'll like to have me play for you, won't you?"

35

The pig rubbed his head into Richard's hand.

"You know something, Runt?" Richard stroked the pig's ears. "I made a mistake about Uncle Ambrose. He *wanted* me to stay with him in Bennington. He really did. There just wasn't anything he could do to keep me."

Aunt Ruth had often said that Richard was a friendly soul. He liked the people he met every day at school and in the store and on the streets of Bennington. Here he seldom saw anyone from outside the farm, except on Sundays. He looked forward to Sundays, when they went to church instead of to the fields. During the long sermons he could wonder about the people in the congregation.

After the service the little children ran around chasing one another. Dan and his friends climbed on the top rail of the fence that surrounded the church and tried to hop along it on one foot, or do handstands or push one another off. The girls their age pretended not to watch. The adults gathered in little groups in the churchyard and the road. The women gossiped and talked about cooking and sewing and their children. The men talked about crops and cattle and prices. Granny Gates and her special friend, Anna, and a few other old ladies stayed inside the church together to catch up on the week's news. Richard stood alone and thought about his friends in Bennington.

Sunday afternoons Richard could do as he pleased, as long as what he wanted to do was quiet. On the first Sunday after his birthday he wanted to write to Uncle Ambrose, but he had neither pen nor ink. There were plenty of quills to be sharpened into pens—on the gander.

I say, Goose, would you be so kind as to give me one of your quills so that I may write a letter to my uncle? He knew how the gander would respond to that!

It turned out not to be a problem at all. Granny had both a quill, which only needed to be sharpened, and ink, which only needed to have water stirred into it. After dinner he headed for the barn with his writing materials.

"Where you going?" Dan asked.

"To the barn. Runt likes company."

"Thought you didn't like pigs."

"Never said that, did I? Besides, Runt likes me."

"Pigs is mighty sociable," Granny cackled. "I had a sow named Pinky when I was a girl. Thought she was a dog. Came when I called. Sat when I said 'sit.' Even taught her to fetch a stick when I threw it. Climbed up into my lap. Was still trying to get in my lap when she weighed more than I did." Granny Gates laughed merrily.

Near the barn door Richard found a smooth board, which he took into the stall with him. As he entered, Runt scrambled up on his back feet with his little front hooves against the side of the trough. He made grunting noises as if to greet Richard.

"Greetings to you, too, Runt. How about a little music before we get down to the business of writing to Uncle Ambrose?"

The boy lifted his recorder from its secret place in the straw, unwrapped it, and sat down on the floor. He'd stolen a few minutes during the week to read Josiah's instructions. While he was working in the field he had tried to remember which holes to cover with his fingers to

37

make certain sounds. Evenings he'd practiced the notes. Now he tried to pick out an easy hymn, "Praise God from Whom All Blessings Flow." When he had figured out the first line, he went on to the second, third, and fourth lines. Then he played the whole hymn straight through.

"Pretty good, wouldn't you say? Do you want to run around out here on the barn floor while I write my letter?"

Richard lifted the pig out onto the floor. Of course Runt had been on the floor before, every time Richard had removed the dirty straw from one corner of the trough and replaced it with clean straw. That was one of the things that surprised Richard about his pig. He dirtied in one corner only, as if he wanted to keep the rest of his bed clean.

Richard spread the paper out on the board. He sharpened the quill with his knife and then he stirred the ink once again.

Dear Uncle Ambrose,

Thank you, thank you for the recorder. I can play "Praise God from Whom All Blessings Flow." If I had more time, I'd be able to play other tunes as well. I am kept very busy.

Richard stopped to think. He'd have to ask Uncle Lyman to mail the letter for him. Since he couldn't trust Uncle Ugly not to read it, he'd best choose his words carefully.

Uncle Lyman and Zeke who is fifteen and the slave named Boy and an ox have pulled all of the stumps from a new field.

Uncle Ambrose would be dismayed when he read that sentence about the slave.

Dan and I loaded a sledge with dung and hauled it out to the field and spread the dung. I can't tell you how many loads we did but it was many. Then they plowed the dung into the dirt. Uncle Lyman told me to plow but I can't plow a straight row so he put me to work picking rocks. I was very stiff from the ride and then from the work. Both hands were blistered. That didn't last long. Now we are planting.

Uncle Lyman says that it is too late in the year for me to start school. Dan doesn't go to school anymore because he is already twelve but since I am still eleven I think he will let me go in the fall.

Uncle Ambrose would not like to read that lie but he would understand—Richard hoped.

I read to the family most nights after supper. Aunt Prudence's mother lives here, too. She is blind and she likes to be read to. Everyone else listens. I am reading *Robinson Crusoe*. Boy has a daughter whose name is Gee Gee. She is a slave, too. She works with Aunt P. I don't know how old she is, about nine, I think.

The day I arrived, Uncle Lyman gave me a newborn pig to "comfort me." I did not like him at first, but I do now.

I miss you. Thank Josiah for the instructions. Say greetings to my friends. Tell them I remember them kindly. Thank you again for the recorder.

Your loving "son,"
Richard Baldwin

He picked up Runt and held his warm little body next to his cheek. Then he carried him out to the pigpen. Zeke came and stood beside them.

"Look at Runt," Richard said. "He was the smallest pig in the litter and now he's as big as the biggest piglet."

"You done good. Saw you had your tooter out. Thought maybe you'd play me a tune."

Richard nodded and they returned to the barn, where Richard played his hymn with only a few mistakes.

"Mighty nice, Dick, but how about something more jolly."

"Like?"

"'Three Ravens Sat on a Tree.' That's a right cheerful tune."

Richard picked out the tune. Zeke, who never talked much, sang with zeal. Zeke was different from his father and his brother.

Late in May Runt's brothers and sisters began going into the woods with their mother to forage for themselves. Runt ate corn and slops. Richard made a harness for him and tied him with a long rope to the barn door. The little pig, who was as big as a small dog, was outside all day but he could come into the barn for shelter. He did his business in a little pile as far from the barn door as the rope would reach. When he was off the rope he followed Richard like a devoted dog.

CHAPTER
6

The first thing every morning during the last week in May, Uncle Lyman had searched the sky. On the fourth morning he announced that all the signs were right for planting corn. It turned out to be a unique day, the day when Richard did a task better than his cousin Dan. The task was dropping seed corn into small holes in hills made of piled-up earth.

Richard punched the holes with a stick. Dan was supposed to drop the seeds. It was difficult for Dan to pick up just three of the tiny kernels. Once he had them between his thumb and fingers, he couldn't hit the target. At least one kernel always landed outside of the hole and then Dan had to struggle to pick it up and put it where it belonged. When Uncle Lyman came to see why they were moving so slowly down the row, Dan's fumbling increased.

"Get those kernels in the hole, Dan!" Uncle Lyman shouted. "Three kernels in each hole. No kernels outside of the hole. We don't have seed corn to waste. Don't have time to waste either."

Dan's hands shook and it took him even longer to pick up the corn. He squatted down so that his hand was close to the top of the hill, but only two kernels landed where they belonged.

Scowling, Uncle Lyman took the stick from Richard and used it to hit Dan across his backside. Then he handed it to Dan. He gave the bag of corn to Richard. "You try it, Dick."

Even though Richard's hands were now callused, he could gather together the kernels and drop them in the center of the hole without difficulty.

"I'm better at everything than you," Dan muttered. "How come you can plant corn?"

"I played the spinet and counted out buttons at the store. I'm used to doing little things with my fingers. You do big things with your arms and shoulders."

"I'm strong," Dan said as he ran ahead, jabbing his stick into the hills as if he hated them.

By the middle of the afternoon there was nothing more for Dan to do; he was sent back to the house. Uncle Lyman and Boy went to the house at suppertime. Richard and Zeke worked until the field was planted, which was almost sundown. For hours Richard had thought how good it would feel to straighten his back, but when he had dropped the last kernels of corn into the last hill, he could not stand straight. He walked bent over like an old lady. Zeke didn't say anything, but he slowed his pace to walk beside him.

"Good work, boys," Uncle Lyman boomed as they entered the house. "I had thought to spend two days planting corn, and we did it all in one day. You were a real help today, Dick." He slapped Richard's sore shoulder and made him wince.

"When do we get our story?" Granny Gates whined.

"Not tonight, Granny," Uncle Lyman said. "Dick did a full day's work—and then some. I expect he'll be ready for sleep as soon as he downs his supper. That right?"

Richard nodded.

"I caught me a nice fish," Dan said. "Ma cooked it for me for supper."

Richard ought to have been happy because Uncle Lyman had praised his work. Instead he envied Dan, who had spent the afternoon sitting under a tree with a fishing rod.

The next Sunday afternoon, Richard sat under a tree with his recorder. Runt splashed in the stream. Gee Gee came and stood under another tree. Her dress was bunched together at the waist with a rope. The skirt had been cut off so that her bare toes peeked beneath it. The sleeves had been cut off above her skinny wrists. She looked pitiful and frail, but Richard knew that she was actually very strong. He had seen her carry heavy rocks, and pails filled with milk or water.

Richard often thought that the slaves were like him, leaves floating downstream with no control over where they went. No one ever asked them what they wanted. What Uncle Lyman said was probably true: the slaves were well cared for, like his animals. They had enough to eat and a place to sleep. They went on from day to day doing what they were told to do. Black Boy—was that the only name he had?—always looked blank, as if shutters had been closed behind his eyes. He never smiled. He never spoke.

"Do you like music?" Richard asked when he came to the end of the hymn he was playing.

Gee Gee nodded.

"Do you sing?"

"No more."

"Do you want me to play another song?"

To his surprise, she shook her head. She rubbed one bare foot against the back of her other leg.

"Do you want to talk?" he asked.

Again she shook her head. "Read. I want to read."

"You don't go to school?"

She shook her head again.

"Do you want to go to school?"

She nodded.

Richard looked away from the little girl and thought hard. Uncle Lyman would not want his slave educated. But everyone should be able to read, and Gee Gee wanted to learn. Furthermore, it would be a pleasure to defy Uncle Ugly secretly. He swept away leaves and rocks to make a smooth space in the dirt. Then he picked up a stick and wrote a letter *G*. "This is a *G* for Gee Gee," he said. "Is that really your name?"

"My name is Georgina."

"So why do they call you Gee Gee?"

"My mother's name is Dina but they called her Girl. I am Girl's girl so they call me Gee Gee."

"And your father? What's his name?"

"He wish he be called George, like George Washington, but he got no name 'cept Black Boy."

"I understand. . . ." He meant to be sympathetic.

She glared at him and stamped her foot. "No you don't."

He stared at her for a few seconds. Then he shrugged his shoulders. "I guess I don't," he whispered. He pointed to the G and wrote the other letters of her name and said them aloud. "What's your surname?"

She looked a question at him.

"Your last name? My last name is Baldwin. Granny's name is Gates. Everyone else is Peck. Lyman Peck and Zeke Peck and Prudence Gates Peck and Dan Peck. Your name is Georgina what?"

She shook her head.

"You don't have a last name?" Could that be? "Maybe someday you can pick your own last name."

Georgina smiled brightly. "Roses be so pretty. I be Georgina Rose." She took the stick from his hand and began to copy the letters.

Richard lifted his recorder and worked on a hymn: "Come, Thou long-expected Jesus, born to set Thy people free."

By the end of the afternoon Georgina could write her name, and Richard could play another hymn.

The next day while he hoed the weeds growing up between the pea plants, Richard thought about ways to teach Georgina the alphabet. When he came into the kitchen for dinner at noon, Georgina was sweeping ashes off the hearth. With his big toe, he traced an *A* in the ashes. She had learned that letter yesterday. Then he traced a *B*. He leaned down as if to ease the stiffness in his neck. "*B*, buh," he whispered.

She copied the *B* with her finger and then swept the letters away, hung up the broom, and picked up her trencher and headed for the door without a smile or even a look in Richard's direction.

That evening Richard carried a full pail of milk into the kitchen. Georgina took it and set it on the worktable behind a smooth sprinkling of flour. Quickly she wrote *A* and *B* with her finger. He added a *C* and whispered the name and sounds of the letter. As Aunt Prudence approached, Georgina pulled the bucket forward to cover the letters.

Richard tried to introduce a new letter or two every day. If they met outside, he scratched a letter in the dirt and told her what it was and how it sounded. Inside, he wrote letters in flour and ashes and batter and butter.

When he finished reading to the family at night, he left the book open on a table near the stairs. Georgina found ways to meet him there so that he could point to letters and short words and whisper them.

The planting was done and eventually it would be time to begin reaping. In the meantime there were weeds to hoe and fences to mend, and trees to fell, and wood to split.

Every day Runt grew bigger and smarter. When he was off his rope he stayed close to Richard, waiting just outside the door when Richard went into the house. In the morning he strained against his harness and made funny little greeting noises as soon as he saw Richard. He was a better pet than any dog Richard had ever heard of.

CHAPTER
7

As soon as they entered the churchyard on the last Sunday in June, Richard noticed that something was different. Greetings were louder; smiles were wider. Nothing special happened during the service but everyone, not just the children, seemed in a hurry to get through the door when the service ended.

As they did every Sunday, Dan and his friends frolicked on the fence and the girls tittered and pretended not to see them. But Granny and her friends came out to the churchyard, where all of the adults were gathered together to discuss a single subject—the Independence Day celebration. The men talked about venison and turkeys and digging a pit for the fire. The women talked about bread and vegetables and pies.

"'Course I'll bring the cannon, same as always," one man said. "Only wish we had a fife so we could have a real parade."

There was silence, even among the children, as everyone thought about a parade.

"Never heard a fife," Zeke drawled. "Sound like Dick's recorder? He can play lots of tunes. I'll bet he could play 'Yankee Doodle.'"

Everyone turned to look at Richard, who nodded. He could teach himself to play "Yankee Doodle."

"Suppose we could make us a couple of drums?" the man with the cannon asked.

"Stretch a hide over a bucket," Zeke said. "Get a couple of sturdy sticks. Dick an' Dan an' me'll bring music."

On Monday before Independence Day, Gee Gee and Aunt Prudence washed. On Tuesday they ironed, but they did not hang all of the clothes upstairs on pegs. They laid best shirts for Uncle Lyman and each of the boys, and dresses for Granny Gates and Aunt Prudence, across the furniture in the parlor so that they would not get wrinkled.

On Wednesday they cooked. Granny shelled peas from the garden. Aunt Prudence baked a maple cake. She sent Richard and Dan out to pick wild strawberries.

"Girl's work," Dan grumbled as they headed to the woods.

Richard had liked to go berry picking with Aunt Ruth, but he didn't say so. As soon as he spotted the first berries, he began to fill his bucket.

Dan picked, too, for a few minutes, and then he jumped to his feet. "Bet you can't do this," he said, as he turned a perfect cartwheel. "Or this." He stood on his head.

Richard didn't try, but went right on picking berries.

"Your head'd go flat if you put all that weight on it."
Dan jumped up and caught hold of a branch and swung
his body in the air. "You'd break this branch."

Richard said nothing and continued to pick berries.
Dan joined him, and they both worked in silence for a bit.

"Look at that turkey over there!" Dan shouted.

Richard turned to where Dan pointed. "Where?" he
asked.

"Blockhead," Dan called. He was running toward the
house with a full bucket of strawberries.

"You stole my berries!" Richard shouted.

Dan turned to face Richard from a distance. "Me? You
saying I cheated you, Dick? Don't say that to Pa. He
wouldn't believe you." He turned back toward the house.

When Richard had filled the second bucket and returned to the house, everyone was sitting down to dinner.

"Don't be discouraged," Uncle Lyman said kindly. "We
don't expect you to do things as quickly as your cousin
yet. He's been raised to work and he has a special knack
for it. It's good that you kept on picking until you had
filled a bucket, even though it took you longer."

With his hands hidden beneath the table, Richard
clenched and unclenched his fists. He wished he could
use his hands to smash Dan's nose right into his freckled
cheeks. Dan smirked. Richard hated him.

As soon as he had finished eating, Richard stomped out
to the barn. He kicked a solid post and then he kicked it
again. "It's not fair, Runt. I could have told Uncle Lyman
that I had picked *both* buckets of berries, but he wouldn't
have believed me. Dan couldn't pick up kernels of corn

with his fumbling fingers; how'd Uncle Ugly think he could pick those little strawberries? When he looks at his boy, Uncle Lyman's as blind as Granny Gates. Like I told you before, Dan's a sneak with a nasty streak. He wants me to look bad."

Runt rubbed against Richard, sympathetically.

Everyone was up early on the Fourth of July. Richard, who had never unpacked his dress-up clothes, took a pair of dark blue velvet breeches from his box and shook out the wrinkles. They were looser around the waist than when he had worn them to Aunt Ruth's funeral. He tried to span his waist with his hands; he was definitely thinner. Was he also taller? He couldn't tell.

"Nice," Gee Gee whispered when he passed her on his way to the breakfast table. She reached out to finger the velvet. *N-I-C-E*, he wrote in a dusting of flour.

Zeke entered the door with a wooden bucket. A smooth hide had been tacked tightly across the top of the bucket. Dan followed with a similar bucket hanging from a rope around his neck. He banged the hide with two thick sticks and grinned.

At last they were ready to go. The three adults sat on the wagon seat. The boys and the food were in the back. Runt ran behind the wagon until his rope held him back. Gee Gee waved from the doorway.

When they reached a house with a small cannon in the front yard, the boys climbed out of the back of the wagon and were greeted by five little children. The oldest carried two pot lids, which he banged together to make a mighty crash.

"Maybe we should practice," Richard suggested.

"We don't need no practice to make a loud noise." Dan laughed.

"Let's practice," Zeke said. "Softly so no one can hear. What'll we do, Dick?"

Richard showed the drummers how to beat out four-four time. *RAT tat Tat tat RAT tat Tat tat*. He suggested that the lid player crash in at the end of every line. "Yankee Doodle went to town"—*crash*. He asked the little children to try to clap at every other drumbeat. *CLAP wait Clap wait CLAP wait Clap wait*.

A little boy, carrying a large flag, led the way. He was followed by three clapping children, then two drummers and the lid player, then Richard, and finally the cannon on a small wagon pulled by two young men. They marched down the road. At the next house they were joined by another group of clapping children and young people. When they turned into a lane leading to a large brick house, everyone began to sing. They stopped in front of tables set up in the center of a broad lawn and played and sang "Yankee Doodle" once again.

Then an old man rose and began to read: "When, in the course of human events . . . all men are created equal . . . they are endowed . . . life, liberty, and the pursuit of happiness." When the reading of the Declaration of Independence was over, the cannon was fired thirteen times, for the thirteen original states.

Then it was time to eat. Richard loaded his pewter plate and looked around for his cousins. Dan was in the midst of a group of boys. One of them pointed at Richard and laughed. Zeke was creeping up toward a pretty girl, who seemed not to know he was there. Richard sat under an elm tree. He got up twice to refill his plate. Then he was so happily stuffed that he leaned back against the rough trunk and closed his eyes.

"Miss Caroline here'd be mighty pleased if you'd play us a tune, Dick."

Richard opened his eyes and smiled at a girl whose dress matched her blue eyes and the ribbon in her curly light hair. "Sorry to wake you, Dick," she whispered.

Zeke set a small log on the grass and motioned for the girl to sit. "Told her you wouldn't mind us wakin' you. Told her you'd like to play for her." His eyes pleaded with Richard. "'Three Ravens Sat on a Tree'?"

"Later, Zeke." Richard pulled his recorder out of his breeches and began to play a beautiful tune called "Greensleeves." Then he played "Three Ravens."

"More!" someone shouted when he stopped playing.

Richard looked up at all the people standing around him and shrugged his shoulders. He played "Praise God" and "Come, Thou Long-Expected Jesus." "I don't know any more songs," he said.

"Just got the tooter this spring," Zeke drawled.

"Well, Lyman," another man called to his uncle, who was still standing at the tables. "Looks like a prize boy here."

"Depends on what you value," Uncle Lyman snapped. "Dick's got no strength—or mind—for working the farm."

"Thank you for playing for us," Miss Caroline whispered.

Zeke patted Richard's shoulder and then put his hand down to help the pretty girl to her feet.

Richard sat on under the elm tree, thinking about what Uncle Lyman had said. *He's right, I'm not good at farm work, except for planting corn.* He remembered how he had dropped a rock so close to Uncle Lyman's foot that he'd almost crippled him, and how he'd fallen flat on his face in the mud. *When I try to plow, my mind wanders off—and so do my furrows. I don't like farm work, and I'll never be as good a farmhand as Dan and Zeke. But, since I'm here, I might just as well try harder to please. . . .*

"Hey Sissy-britches!" A boy named Tom, one of Dan's friends, suddenly pulled the recorder out of his hand and threw it to another boy. Then he yanked Richard to his feet. "Bet you got lace sewed to your drawers and vest. Hear you sleep in a nightshirt." He punched Richard on the shoulder. "Sissy." He punched him again, harder.

The boy was daring Richard to fight. Richard had never tried to fight. "Only ruffians fight," Aunt Ruth had said.

Uncle Ambrose had said that there were two kinds of fights. One was just brawling with no purpose but to humiliate or hurt someone. The other was for a worthwhile cause. Fighting for independence was good because the cause was noble.

This boy was humiliating Richard with words. If he were to raise his fists, the boy would hurt him. Richard did the only thing he knew to do; he turned and ran.

"Sissy-britches! Sissy-britches!" Boys' voices sang like a chorus.

Richard's ears burned as he ran. He didn't know how many boys were chasing him. He ran until his sides hurt and his knees began to quiver. He would have to drop to the ground and surrender to the pack. He staggered, expecting to fall. Instead, two warm hands grabbed his shoulders and propelled him into the house. He looked up into a smiling black face.

"Sit in there and catch your breath." The woman pointed to an open doorway.

He stumbled through it and dropped onto a chair. When he was no longer gasping for breath, he looked toward the door, but the woman had gone. Then he looked around him. The floor was covered with a large, many-colored rug. There were pictures on the walls and a bouquet of flowers on a polished table. In the corner by a window was a pianoforte!

Tense with wonder, Richard crept toward it. He must not touch it. He clasped his hands behind his back but . . . Just one note. He reached out with one finger and touched the F-sharp. One more? He touched the G.

"Pull out the stool, boy, and try it out."

Richard clasped his hands together and turned, terrified. In the doorway a spindly old woman stood with a pitcher in her hand. He had seen her many times at church.

"Is it yours?" Richard breathed.

"It is. If you know how to play it, sit down and play."

Richard played the theme from Handel's Air with Variations and a Mozart minuet, surprised that his fingers still remembered the patterns. He leafed through the music on the rack and picked out other melodies.

When he had finished, he heard another sound—clapping. Startled, he looked around. The spindly woman was seated in an easy chair behind him. The colored woman stood in the doorway. The clapping had come from the people who were leaning in the open windows and the others who were standing behind them.

"Didn't I tell you, Anna, that the boy has a gift?" Granny Gates shouted to her deaf friend.

"He sits the stool nice!" Anna shouted back.

Richard grinned and then he turned to his hostess. "Thank you," he said. That wasn't enough. "It's been . . . I have missed . . . I . . ." He could not find the right words.

She rose and took his hand in both of hers. "I thank you, Richard. My husband loved this instrument. It has been a pleasure to hear you play it. I hope you will come often." She turned to the window. "There's still lots of food. Let's eat it."

When she left the room, the black woman entered it with a boy who was about Richard's height but thinner. His eyes were like raisins in skin the color of maple sugar. "Name's Caleb," he said. "Doubt old Peck will let you come visit us, but maybe you and me can stop here on the way home from school and you can teach me. Mr.

Bristol taught me the notes before he died, but my fingers get all twisted. You've had real lessons."

"I'd be pleased. . . ."

"Dick, get out here." Uncle Lyman sounded angry.

Richard was passing through the doorway when Caleb's mother put her hand on his arm. "Georgina and Boy? Tell them Mary—that's me—and Jacob—that's my man—we're grieving right along with them. You tell them that? Now you hurry on. Lyman Peck, he won't want you talkin' to us that Master Bristol made free. We stick in his craw." She smiled as if to say that she was happy to stick in Uncle Lyman's craw.

Richard walked slowly toward the wagon, searching the ground for his recorder. He couldn't leave until he found it.

"Pick up your feet, Dick!" Uncle Lyman shouted.

"My recorder. I have to find—"

"Get in the wagon. Now." Uncle Lyman flicked the back of his legs with the whip he used on the horses.

"Tooter's safe," Zeke whispered, and reached his hand down from the back of the wagon to pull Richard up beside him.

When he jumped down from the wagon, Richard's legs still stung where Uncle Lyman had flicked them with his whip. Runt greeted him with happy grunts. Richard went to him and the pig raised himself with his front hooves against the boy's leg.

"Missed me, didn't you?" Richard scratched him between his ears and thought that the pig would have wagged his tail if he'd had a waggable one.

"Help the boys unhitch, Dick, and unload the wagon. Hear me?" These were the first words Uncle Lyman had spoken since they had left the Bristol farm. He was cross; Richard didn't know why.

When the tasks were done, Richard took Runt to the stream to splash for a moment before the farm was completely enveloped in the blackness of night. On his way back to the house, he knocked on the door to the slaves' lean-to and delivered Mary's message to Georgina's father, who listened with the shutters still closed over his eyes.

Georgina was leading Granny Gates through the door into her room as Richard entered the kitchen. "That you, Richard?" the old lady asked. "Wanted to thank you for the music today. As I told Anna, it's a real treat—"

"Good night, Granny." Uncle Lyman banged his fist on the table in front of him. "You, Dick, stand here in front of me and listen, listen good. You think you're a dandy or something in your velvet breeches?"

"No, sir."

"I don't want to see 'em again. As for all this music making, it's sissy. Sissy." He banged the table again.

"Mrs. Bristol told me that her husband played the pianoforte," Richard whispered, and then trembled. He'd have been wiser to keep his mouth shut.

"Old Mr. Bristol thought he was better than the rest of us. He put on airs. Brick house with mowed grass and flowers around it, fancy furniture. He sent his boy to that sissified Harvard College. Didn't do him no good. The boy was killed in the battle at Albany."

Uncle Lyman paused and then went on. "Still thought he was Solomon, always comin' out here to preach at me about my slaves. He wanted to free his, that was his business. He could afford to free them. I need Boy and I need my own boys and I need you. I'm feeding you. Don't you forget that. You think about farming, not music. No more showing off like today. Understand?"

Richard nodded and then froze when Uncle Lyman rose from the table with the recorder in his hand. He must have been hiding it on the chair beside him. He walked to the fireplace with it and thrust it toward the flames.

"No!" the boy cried. "Please, Uncle Lyman. Please don't burn it."

"Why not? You don't care about this tooter. You wouldn't even fight for it. You ran away from a fight. You shamed me. Zeke got it back."

Richard stood biting his lip, trying to think of the right thing to say.

At last Uncle Lyman turned away from the fireplace to glare at Richard. He still had the recorder in his hand. "Tell you what. I'll put it right here over the fireplace where you can see it every day. Come winter when we don't have so many chores, I might give it back to you. Till then, there'll be no more music making. Hear me?"

"Yes, sir," Richard said sadly.

As he turned away from his uncle, Richard saw Georgina standing in the doorway to Granny Gates's room. She scurried across the kitchen and outside. Richard followed her.

"Where do you think you're going?" Uncle Lyman yelled.

"To the privy," Richard yelled back.

CHAPTER

8

Richard had little time to miss his recorder. He was harvesting—oats and rye and clover and wheat and finally corn. Every day except Sunday or when it rained, Uncle Lyman would give Richard a knife or a scythe and tell him where to work. His final instructions were always the same: "Keep up with Dan."

Impossible. Richard tried, but he never cut as much grain as Dan. He went to bed exhausted and woke up tired. There was no time for reading.

Runt had to fend for himself. All day he roamed free, taking himself to the stream or to the field where Richard was working.

"Do you understand that you are a pig, not a dog?" Richard often asked Runt.

Of course, he imagined Runt responding. I'm not only bigger than a dog, I'm smarter.

Richard agreed. Runt was one smart creature; loving, too.

Whenever he could, Richard stole time to help

Georgina with her reading. One day, while they were hoe-ing the garden, he scratched a sentence between the rows of beans. "The fat cat sat on the rat."

"The f-f-f-f-at-fat c-c-c-c-at-cat sat on the rat." Georgina read aloud and then she laughed.

Richard laughed, too. "That's great, Georgina," he said. It pleased him to think how angry Uncle Lyman would be if he were to hear his slave child read.

Granny Gates was the only person with time. She was also the only person who dared speak her mind to Uncle Lyman. "Let's hear a tune on your tooter, Richard," she said as they finished their dinner on the last Sunday in August. "Then we'll have a story."

"I'm sorry, Granny . . ." Richard looked at his uncle to finish the sentence.

"Dick is a farmer, not a music man." Uncle Lyman banged his fist on the table.

"It's Sunday. He's not farming today. We've had no music and no readin' most of this summer." Granny Gates turned her clouded eyes toward Uncle Lyman and then toward Richard. "Get the tooter," she said. "You can play hymns, since it's the Lord's Day."

"The boy will not be making music today or any other day this summer so quit your pestering, Granny." Uncle Lyman got up from the table.

"You're a cruel man, Lyman," she hissed. "Me that is blind wants music. Him that is a poor orphan wants to make music. Get your tooter, Richard."

Richard looked from one to the other.

"Just this once?" Aunt Prudence begged "To please Granny?"

"No!" Uncle Lyman shouted, and headed for the door.

"Could I read to her, please?" Richard asked boldly.

"You may not touch the tooter, but you can waste your time readin'—or you can ride over to the Stony Kill and go fishin' with me and the boys. Choose for yourself."

Richard went up to the loft and took a book from his box. It was the only book written especially for children that he had brought with him. Aunt Ruth and Uncle Ambrose had sent to Boston for this copy of *Puss in Boots* and had given it to him for his eighth birthday. He still loved it and was sorry that he could not share the pictures of the cat in tall boots with Granny.

Even though it was a children's book, Granny responded properly. "Poor boy," she said when he read about the miller leaving his third son nothing but a cat. She gasped when the cat killed the rabbit and smiled when he took the rabbit to the king. She sighed happily when the clever cat had succeeded in helping his master become a prince.

Aunt Prudence, who had sat down beside Richard so that she could see the pictures as he read, smiled for a moment and then slapped the table with her hand. "What could a body learn from that story? Don't either of you tell the menfolk about it. On the Lord's Day we read the Bible, if we read at all."

"Thank you, Richard," Granny said. "While you were reading I forgot how hot it is today. I'm remembering now."

Richard went outside and called to Runt. It had been

hot and dry for so long that the stream was only a trickle. Nevertheless, they waded in the little water that remained. When his feet were cold, Richard sat under a tree with his book on his knees. If it was proper to fish on Sunday, why wasn't it also proper to read a story? He heard a noise and turned to see Georgina peering through the leaves of a dusty bush.

"Come join us," Richard said. "Uncle Lyman and the boys have gone fishing, so we don't have to worry about being caught. I wanted to ask you if you know when school starts. Should be pretty soon now. Maybe when the corn is harvested?"

Georgina laughed. "You going to teach the school? There ain't nothin' for you to learn."

"There isn't anything," he corrected her.

"Everybody here say, 'there ain't nothin'.' Do it make a difference?"

"Yes, it *does*, Georgina. Educated people speak well."

"Won't never make no difference to me. You be the only educated person I know."

"'It won't make a difference to me. You are the only educated person I know.' That's what you should have said."

"So why you want to go to school when already you know so much?"

"To learn more," Richard said. "To learn enough so that I could go to college and learn even more."

Georgina clapped her hands and laughed. "Ain't— aren't you the one, Master Richard?"

Richard jumped up and glared at Georgina. "Don't you

ever, ever call me master. I am not your master. I will never be any person's master. Do you understand that, Georgina? There are people, lots of people, who think owning slaves is sinful. I am one of those people."

She smiled and shrugged her shoulders. "So be the Bristol folks in the big brick house. Mr. Bristol be mighty mad if he know that Mr. Lyman sold my mama. Send her south. Say he need money. Say I can do my mama's work. I wear my mama's dresses. They all so big." She sighed and turned away.

"You miss your mother, don't you?" he said.

"Me and Pa. Pa, he say he ain't never goin' to talk to Mr. Lyman again. And he ain't . . . he hasn't? He mighty mad."

"But your father works hard."

"What else? He don't work, he be sold and sent far, far away. Mama never find him."

"How long has she been gone?"

"More than a year. She cry and cry. She hang on to the barn door so it take three men to drag her away. They put a . . ." Georgina put her thumb and forefinger around her ankle so that Richard could picture the slave in an ankle chain.

Richard handed Georgina the book he had read to Granny and watched her face as she examined the picture of the cat in the tall boots. She laughed out loud, and then she began to read. Richard helped her with words she did not know and then read the last pages to her.

"Take it to your room and study it," he said, putting the book in her hands.

She looked frightened and tried to give it back to him. "I can't," she said over and over.

"Yes you can. For a time. When you know all the words, you can give it back to me."

October came and the trees began to turn color. The harvests were complete. Richard was once again reading to the family in the evenings after supper.

Still there was no mention of school until Richard introduced the subject himself. "I've been thinking about school," he said to Uncle Lyman one night when Aunt Prudence had taken Granny Gates off to her room. "When will the fall session start?"

Uncle Lyman did not reply, but sat for a long time twisting his mustache. Then he went to the fireplace and picked up the recorder and set it down in front of Richard.

The boy reached out a finger to stroke the smooth wood. "Thank you, Uncle Lyman."

"I despair for you, Dick." Uncle Lyman twisted his mustache again. "Know what makes this country great? It's land. A body could go west, even out beyond the Ohio territory, and what'd he find? Land. Our great men are all farmers. George Washington, may he rest in peace, was a farmer. And Thomas Jefferson . . ."

"Benjamin Franklin wasn't a farmer," Richard inserted, and then realized that it was a mistake to correct Uncle Lyman.

"And you argue. If I said the moon was shining, you'd tell me it was the sun. What are you going to do with your life? Sit around playing tunes and reading and talking. How're you going to feed your stomach? Answer me that. And don't tell me you don't need food. I've seen how much you eat."

"I could be a storekeeper, or a teacher. . . ."

"Or a preacher, I suppose. You ever feel the call to preach the gospel, Dick?"

Richard shook his head. "No, but I could be a schoolmaster, if I were smart enough. . . ."

"Nothing wrong with your head except that you use it for dreaming instead of working."

"But I'd need an education."

"You can read and figure. What more does a body need?"

Richard didn't try to answer the question aloud. Uncle Lyman would never understand that there were degrees of reading and figuring, or that there were other subjects to study.

"You think the common school here has anything for you? I saw the new schoolmaster down at the mill. Looks like a rope, shoulders no broader than his rump, skin white, spine like jelly. And whiny. Thirty children is too much. Not enough desks. He asked about the older boys. Said they should be in school learning Greek. Who needs Greek? Answer me that."

Greek! Richard bit his lip so that he would not answer hastily. He longed to study Greek. He'd need it if he was ever to go to college. "Did the schoolmaster say if he went to a college?"

"Someplace off the other side of Albany. Good farmland

out there, I hear. I asked him why he ain't planting the soil, and you know what he said? He said he's planting ideas. That calf gave *me* a regular sermon all about ideas. Too many ideas floatin' around already. That's what I told him. Go to bed, Dick."

Richard went but he did not sleep for a long time. Instead he tried to think of something he could do or say so that Uncle Lyman would let him go to school. He remembered the afternoon when he had fallen in the mud and been sent to the house. He remembered another day when he had planted corn while Dan had gone fishing. For a long time he lay awake scheming. Then he closed his eyes and prayed that his scheme would work.

CHAPTER 9

After breakfast the next day they went out to work on the new roof for the barn. On the ground, Uncle Lyman and Zeke cut shingles from blocks of wood. The old roof was made of bark which the two younger boys were expected to rip off before they hammered the new shingles into place. Richard climbed up the ladder behind Dan. When he reached the roof he slipped and kicked the ladder to the ground. He threw his body against the old roof. Uncle Lyman and Zeke came running.

"Don't worry," Richard called down to them. "I'm not hurt." He began to rip up the old bark and throw it down. A piece hit Uncle Lyman's head. "Sorry," Richard called. "I wish I weren't so clumsy."

"We all wish you weren't so clumsy, Dick." Uncle Lyman sighed and returned to the work of splitting shingles.

Richard liked being on the roof. He could see out over the countryside to the next farm. Boy was working with the ox just beyond the farthest field, loading huge rocks onto a sledge and pulling them to one side. During the winter they would cut the trees; in the spring they would pull the stumps and plant an additional field.

Richard sang as he pulled up the old shingles. He sang as he hammered the new ones into place.

"Enough of that bawlin'," Uncle Lyman said as he climbed up on the roof beside the boys. And then he swore. "What do you call that? I showed you how to shingle. Dan showed you how to shingle. You know you're supposed to overlap the shingles evenly. Look at that row. A five-year-old girl could do better than that. Where's your head, Dick? Rip that row out and do it right. I do believe that you are . . . you are . . . the bumblingest boy in the whole state."

Richard's plan was working perfectly! He kept his smile inside and worked slowly for the rest of the day. From time to time he sang a few notes and then stopped in the middle of a line. That annoyed most people. I am being devious, devilishly devious, he said to himself proudly.

Toward the end of the day he dropped his hammer so that it clattered down the slope of the roof and crashed on a rock just feet from a cow that had been tethered outside.

"Hopeless!" Uncle Lyman shouted. "Get down from that roof before you scare us out of our britches, Dick. Maybe your aunt has a job for you. Maybe she needs wood. Think you could carry wood without dropping it on your toes?"

Richard scampered down the ladder. When he was almost to the ground, he remembered to stumble.

74

"I'm just so useless," he mumbled as if to himself but loud enough for Uncle Lyman to hear.

The next day Uncle Lyman sent Zeke up on the roof with Dan. "Maybe Dick'll be able to cut shingles better than he can nail them into place," he said, sighing.

"I hope so," Richard said, "but I know I won't be as good as Zeke. Your boys are such good workers."

Uncle Lyman peered into Richard's face and raised an eyebrow.

Careful, Richard warned himself. If he were *too* clumsy or if he praised his cousins *too* much, Uncle Lyman would catch on to his scheme.

All day Richard worked carefully, but very slowly. Late in the afternoon, the tool he was using slipped and cut his finger.

"Clumsy, clumsy, clumsy!" Uncle Lyman shouted as he yanked at both ends of his mustache. "Go inside and ask Prudence to wrap your finger. Then carry in a load of wood."

"Why's Dick going to the house?" Dan called from the roof. "'Taint quittin' time, is it?"

"The three of us work better without him," Uncle Lyman snarled.

True, Richard said to himself, being careful not to smile. You won't even miss me while I'm learning Greek.

The new schoolmaster was at church on Sunday. Uncle Lyman was right: he did look like a rope. His shoulders were narrow, his neck and his face and his skinny legs were long.

As they were leaving the church after the service, Mrs. Bristol tapped Richard on the shoulder. "You haven't been to play the pianoforte," she said. "I didn't expect you during harvest, but I surely expected you to be attending school. I looked for you all week. Now I hear you haven't been to school."

"No, ma'am, I just discovered that school has started."

"Lyman didn't tell you?" Without waiting for an answer she turned and hurried toward Uncle Lyman. "I say, Lyman," she called so that everyone stopped talking and looked first at her and then at him. "Why aren't your boys in school? We have a fine new schoolmaster, straight out of Union College. Lots of little children, of course, but our Caleb needs company, boys his own age."

"Caleb's no company for my boys. You know that." Uncle Lyman scowled. "My boys can read and figure. They don't need no more." He climbed into his wagon and shouted to his family. "Enough jawing. It's time to go home."

Aunt Prudence scurried to Granny Gates's side and ushered her away from her friend. Zeke backed away from the pretty girl named Caroline. Dan did a handstand on the fence and then flipped to the ground and jumped into the wagon.

Uncle Lyman didn't speak all the way home. He said a short grace and then he didn't speak all during dinner. When the last crumbs of gingerbread had disappeared he turned to Dan. "Want to go to school, Dan?" he asked.

Dan stared at his father for a moment and then he scowled so that Richard thought how much alike they

76

were. "Me? Go to school? Why? Don't have that roof on the barn yet. I know how to add and subtract and read. Please, Pa. Don't make me go to school no more."

For the first time that day, Uncle Lyman smiled. "You're a fine lad," he said, reaching over to pat his arm. "And you, Dick, are you going to be smart like your cousin?"

Richard hadn't planned for this. He tried to think quickly, knowing that a false word might ruin his chances. "I envy Dan," he said slowly. "He can do anything that needs doing around the farm and he's fast, too. He's already a good farmer, whereas I don't know as I'll ever get the knack of it. I'm a bumbler, a terrible bother. . . ."

"Don't say such things, Richard," Granny spoke up. "We're all mighty glad to have you. And you read and I like that and—"

"Hush, Granny. Let the boy speak for himself." Uncle Lyman fingered his mustache. "Go on, Dick."

"An education might help me find a position where I wouldn't always be dependent on kind people like you. Besides, if you sent me to school, I'd be out from under your feet during the day for a few months."

"That's true enough." Uncle Lyman laughed. "Start school if you want, but mind, you'll have to walk. I don't want to hear no whimpering when the snows come. You want to go to school, you go every day, no matter the weather. And you keep the woodbox full here at home." He rose from the table and stood between his sons, clapping each of them on a shoulder. "Let's the three of us saddle up and ride over Lambert's way. Don't think Zeke here saw enough of their pretty li'l Caroline today."

Zeke's face turned as red as an apple.

"What's this about Zeke and Caroline?" Granny Gates asked. "Nobody ever tells me nothing. You sweet on Caroline, Zeke?"

Zeke swallowed. He said nothing.

"Let's read some psalms, shall we Granny?" Richard said, and was rewarded with one of Zeke's slow smiles.

The next morning Richard whistled under his breath as he hurried toward the road in the gray misty dawn. Once he was on the road and out of earshot of the house, he threw back his head. "Forth in thy name, O Lord, I go, my daily labor to pursue," he sang loudly, joyfully. He looked up at the trees, ahead toward a bend in the road, and then back. Runt was trotting behind him.

Richard sighed and turned back to the farm. The pig followed him and stood quietly while Richard tied the rope to his halter. "You really don't want to go to school," Richard told him as he scratched the pig's head. Then he called up to Zeke, who was working on the barn roof, and asked him to release Runt later in the morning.

He ran to make up for the time he had lost taking Runt home. When his sides began to hurt, he slowed to a walk and hummed "Three Ravens" under his breath. The sun was sweeping away the mist, and Richard was going to school. It was a beautiful morning! The road was long, five miles Dan had said, and hilly. He patted the recorder in his pocket. Maybe he could play it while he walked home at a slower pace.

He had just passed the lane to the Bristol house when he heard the bell that announced the opening of the school day. He began to run. The schoolmaster stood in front of the little cabin with the bell in his hand. Small children walked single file past him and through the door.

"A new student," the young man who looked like a rope called to him. "Welcome."

"Thank you," Richard panted, and wiped his sleeve across his sweaty forehead. "Name's Richard Baldwin. Do you really know Greek?"

"Yes. Do you?"

"No, sir."

"But you want to learn it?"

"Yes, sir."

"And why would that be?"

"I'd planned to go to college. That is my uncle—not the uncle I'm living with now, but my uncle in Bennington—had planned for me to go to the academy and then to college."

The schoolmaster nodded and ushered Richard through the door. "My name is Dewey, Jonathan Dewey." He looked around the little room. "You mind crowding in there beside Caleb?"

"No, sir."

Caleb greeted him with a grin. "Been wondering where you were," he whispered.

Later, while they were eating their lunches, Caleb told Richard that his parents had built their house on land that Mr. Bristol had given them many years ago. His two older brothers and their father farmed their land as well as the Bristol land. His mother helped Mrs. Bristol in her house.

After school Richard stopped at the Bristol house and played a Mozart piece on the pianoforte and then he helped Caleb with it. As he was leaving, Caleb's mother gave him a piece of pie, which he ate as he walked along at a brisk pace. When he finished the pie, he walked faster to make up for the time he had spent at Mrs. Bristol's. He thought about Caleb, who didn't shout or do tricks. He didn't brag. He looked Richard straight in the eye and he smiled a lot. Richard liked him.

Halfway up the last hill, Richard stopped to catch his breath and saw Runt running toward him. "You're as awkward as I am," he called to his pig, "but my body is not as fat anymore, and my legs are longer."

When they met, Runt rubbed his body against Richard's thigh. As they walked home together, the boy told the pig about school. "Caleb and I will study geometry together; we'll study geography and history with the three oldest girls. Caleb's not interested in Greek because he's not planning to go to college. He's going to be a blacksmith. I'm the only one who will study Greek; Mr. Dewey will teach me when he has time." Richard scratched the first four letters of the Greek alphabet into the dirt. "Isn't that something?" he asked his pig.

Runt responded with a grunt.

"I'll race you home," Richard said as he began to run. "Uncle Lyman will be mad if I don't get the woodbox filled before supper."

No one except Granny Gates asked Richard about school. It didn't matter; Runt came along the road to meet Richard every afternoon. Runt seemed to like to hear about school.

CHAPTER

10

It was raining, not just a sprinkle but a real downpour, when Richard woke one morning of the second week.

"Dick'll drown if he goes off on a day like this, Lyman," Aunt Prudence whispered. "Couldn't he ride one of the horses?"

"He can stay home and help us cut shingles in the barn if he's too delicate to walk," Uncle Lyman replied.

"Will you stay home, Dick?" Aunt Prudence asked when her husband had left the house.

"Dick won't want to get wet. Dick's a sissy." Dan laughed as he followed his father out to the barn.

Richard rose from the table and lifted his heavy woolen coat from the peg by the door and put it on.

Zeke came and lifted his oilskin cape from its peg and draped it over the heavy coat. It was so long that Richard knew it would keep him dry from his shoulders to the tops of his thick boots.

"Won't you need it?" he asked.

"Not as much as you." Zeke left the room before Richard had a chance to thank him properly.

Late in the week there was a light dusting of snow and the air turned cold. Caleb told Richard that Mrs. Bristol was expecting him to sleep at her house whenever the weather was bad. "She said you might just as well plan to move in for the winter months." Richard did not mention the invitation to Uncle Lyman, but it pleased him.

It was light when he left Mrs. Bristol's house but darkness seemed to creep ever earlier. By November it was so dark that Richard often felt Runt's snout against his leg before he saw the pig.

On an evening early in December, when the wind was so cold it bit right through Richard's coat and shirt, Runt did not come to meet him. Must be too cold even for Runt, Richard said to himself as he pushed his numb hands deeper into his pockets and snuggled his chin down into his collar. When he could see the light in the kitchen window up ahead, he called to Runt.

Where could he be? Richard began to run toward the house as he remembered the excitement in Dan's voice that morning. It was butchering day, Dan had said. Richard, who had been groggy with sleep, had thought only of the pigs that had been brought in from the woods. Some had been herded off to be sold; others had been penned and fed with corn for the last several weeks. They were the pigs to be butchered to supply the family with meat. Perhaps Runt had been frightened and had run away to hide. He called again.

"Hi there, Dick!" Dan yelled. "Heard you calling that pig you thought was a dog. You know where he is? He's right here." Dan lifted a lantern to illuminate five skinned bodies hanging from a tree in the barnyard.

Richard felt sick; his legs turned to jelly. In spite of the cold, his face began to burn; he couldn't breathe.

"This here fat one is your Runt." Dan poked a carcass so that it swung slowly to and fro, to and fro. "He'll be the tastiest one of the bunch. He was the easiest to catch. Came right up to me when I called him."

Richard ran into the barn, to the empty stall that had been Runt's home. He threw himself down on the floor and buried his head between his knees. How? Why? Uncle Lyman had given the pig to him. He'd never said anything about taking him back, or killing him. Dan said that Runt had come when he was called—because he'd been taught to trust people. If only he'd run away!

Someone came into the stall and sat down beside him. "Raised a lamb once," Zeke muttered. Richard didn't respond, and they sat in silence for a while. "Got to go finish the milkin'." Zeke got to his feet. "Sorry, Dick."

Tears rose in Richard's eyes and he didn't try to stop them, or the sobs that convulsed his chest.

"Stop bawlin' like a baby." Uncle Lyman prodded his rump with the toe of his boot. "You think I can feed a useless hog over the winter? We raise pigs to eat and to sell to others to eat, not for company. If you'd had any sense you'd have known that. Get up and act like a man." He kept prodding until Richard rose to his feet.

Uncle Ugly was *smiling*. Richard lifted his hand, and

made a fist. And then he dropped it. He could not hit his uncle!

When Uncle Lyman returned to the house, Richard dropped down onto the floor of the stall again. He was cold and numb with grief. Nothing good lasts, he said over and over to himself, remembering Aunt Ruth and their rooms over the store in Bennington.

I'm like a leaf floating in a stream, Richard thought sadly. I don't have any control over my destination. Uncle Lyman makes the decisions and I do what he says. But not for always! One day, I'll leave Uncle Ugly's ugly farm. I'll never come back!

The barn door opened. Georgina called to him and then brought a trencher of food and set it on the floor beside him. She patted his arm and disappeared. As he sat there, Richard wondered about Georgina. Most likely she hated Uncle Ugly as much as he did, but she and her father would *never* leave the farm—unless they were sold. That could be worse than staying. They could be sold separately and never see each other again, just as the slave they called Girl had been sold. They might not have enough to eat or warm clothes. There was no better life ahead for Georgina and Boy. Maybe it was better to be dead than to live without hope that things would be better.

When only the embers of the fireplace lighted the window in the kitchen, Richard crept to the house. He clung to the edge of the bed so that no part of his body would touch Dan.

A huge fire was burning under a kettle in the barnyard

when Richard went to the privy the next morning. He did not look toward the bodies hanging in the tree.

In the kitchen, Uncle Lyman glared at him. "I'd thought to have your help today, scraping the hides. We need every hand to cut up the meat and set it to smoking and to clean the entrails and stuff them with sausage. But you wouldn't be of help. Better to have you out of the way." He got up from the table and headed out of doors.

"I'll save you one of Runt's ears," Dan laughed as he poked Richard in the ribs. "He's goin' to be tastier than the others 'cause he was raised on food from the kitchen and the fields. He's fat and tender, just like you, Dick." Dan slapped him on the back.

Richard was so angry that his whole body trembled. He rose from the table, lifted his coat off the peg, and headed for school, even though it was still dark outside. He walked along beneath a cloud of sadness. He sat on the school steps until Mr. Dewey arrived to open the door.

"Something's wrong, Richard," Mr. Dewey said. "Is there anything I can do to help?"

Richard just shook his head.

After school he helped Caleb learn a new piece but he did not play the instrument himself.

Day after day Richard mourned for all the losses in his life. Walking home from school in the darkness, he would hear a sound and think—for just a moment—that it was Runt running out to greet him. And then he would remember and try to shut out the picture of his pig hanging in the tree. He never ate pork, even when Uncle

Lyman assured him that the meat was not from Runt. He couldn't trust Uncle Lyman.

"I swear, Dick," Uncle Lyman said to him one evening. "You're as sulky as Boy. Used to think we'd never get you to quit talkin' and singin'. Seems like you hardly ever have anything to say these days. You're not even playing your tooter."

That wasn't true, of course. Richard sometimes played his recorder as he walked the road to or from school. His songs were always sad and slow. He read to the family most evenings.

Mr. Dewey kept him after school one afternoon. "Your work is first rate, Richard. You're learning Greek, and you're patient with the little ones. But something is not right with you. I know you've had some tough knocks. Your mother and your aunt had died and you had moved here from Bennington long before I met you. You seemed to be fairly contented then, and eager to learn. Do you want to tell me what's wrong?"

Richard shook his head. The schoolmaster would never understand how he felt about a pig.

"Tell me, Richard. What was the happiest day or event you can remember?"

Richard thought a minute and then he had to smile. "When I was ten, before Aunt Ruth got sick, Uncle Ambrose closed the store and the three of us took the stage all the way to Boston. We went to two concerts. On Sunday we went to Kings Chapel."

"It's a beautiful church."

"With an organ. A pipe organ that sounds like all the instruments in the world."

"That's a fine memory, isn't it? Now, tell me, Richard, what is the happiest thing that you can dream of happening in the future?"

"Living in Boston so I could hear that organ every Sunday. I'd be the best churchgoer in all Boston. And maybe . . ."

"You could play that organ? Or another organ."

"Uncle Ambrose said there is an organ in Philadelphia."

"True. A man named David Tannenberg is building organs in Pennsylvania. But there are organs not far from here, two in churches in Albany and one at Saint George's Church in Schenectady. I know the man who plays that one."

"Schenectady's not far from Albany. When I run away—" Richard clapped his hand over his mouth.

"When you are ready to set off on your own, you could go to Schenectady and learn to play the organ while you are attending Union College."

Richard bit his lip. "I don't see how that's possible, sir," he whispered. "Uncle Lyman would think that was a waste of money. He thinks everyone should farm. I couldn't ask Uncle Ambrose; he's not really my flesh-and-blood uncle. He hasn't written to me for a very long time. He's most likely forgotten about me. . . ."

"So you'd work. Why do you think I am out here teaching school? So I can earn money so I can study law.

You're not lazy or you wouldn't be walking ten miles every day to attend school."

Richard couldn't say anything, but he knew he was grinning.

"It makes you happy to think about what might be: playing an organ, going to college, living among people who like music and books. The past is past. It might be a good idea for you to try not to think about it. If your present isn't happy, you can at least use it to prepare for the future—which will be as you make it."

His talk with Mr. Dewey made Richard feel better. He could not forget Runt, but every time a picture of the pig came into his mind, he replaced it with a picture of himself making music on a huge organ. That picture made him smile. Besides, he was sure that life with Uncle Lyman couldn't get any worse. He was wrong about that.

Late one afternoon in January he finished his session at the pianoforte with Caleb, ate a piece of gingerbread, and set out from the Bristol house at a brisk pace. Although the air was cold there was still a trace of sun, and he knew that if he hurried he could be almost home before dark.

Uncle Lyman's wagon was drawn across the Bristol lane at the point where it entered the town road. Richard waved and ran at top speed toward the wagon.

"Thanks for waiting to give me a ride, Uncle Lyman," he said as he climbed up onto the seat. "You been down to the mill?" When he turned to look at his uncle's face, he felt as if he had been hit in the stomach.

Uncle Lyman was holding the reins so tightly that his

knuckles were white. His teeth were clenched. His eyes were on fire. "So it's true. You go to the Bristol place every afternoon. I heard that at the mill this afternoon, but I didn't believe it. I gave you permission to go to school. That's the only place I gave you permission to go. So what have you been doing in there? Playing the piano—like a girl?"

Richard wanted to tell his uncle that playing the piano was not a girlish thing to do, but he didn't. He just nodded.

"They say you sit with Caleb. Darky don't know his place. Next thing you'll be tellin' me that *he* plays the piano, too."

Richard said nothing.

"So hear me and hear me good. No more. No more sitting with that darky."

"There aren't any empty desks," Richard whispered.

"Then tell the darky to sit on the floor. And tell that teacher that I won't have *my* kin sittin' with no heathen African. And don't you never go to the Bristol place again unless I tell you you can go. Now get out of the wagon. I told you if you wanted to go to school you'd walk both ways, both ways every day!"

Richard ran almost all of the way to school the next morning to be there early. He went right inside and up to Mr. Dewey's table. What he had to say was so difficult that he blurted it out quickly, to get the saying of it over with. "My uncle told me to tell you that I can't sit with Caleb anymore. I'm sorry, sir. It's just that . . ."

"I've been expecting this. I hear your uncle has slaves.

How do you feel about slavery in general and Caleb in particular, Richard?"

"My uncle in Bennington said slavery is wrong. He wrote pieces for the paper about people owning other people."

"And you agree with your Bennington uncle?"

"Yes, sir, I do. Caleb is my friend. I don't know how I'm going to tell him. . . . I can't go to Mrs. Bristol's anymore either."

"I hear that one of your uncle's slaves is just a child. She should be in school, shouldn't she?"

"She'd like to be going to school, but I'm teaching her to read. She's learning real fast."

"What does your uncle think about that?"

"He doesn't know."

"And the other slave is her father? What does he say?"

"He doesn't say anything. He doesn't talk."

"He can't talk?"

"I don't know. I think he quit talking when Uncle Lyman sold Georgina's mother."

"And where is Georgina's mother now? Does anyone know?"

Richard shook his head. "Georgina doesn't know."

Mr. Dewey rubbed his hand along his jaw. "It's a sad world, isn't it, Richard? Move that bench up here. You can sit at the end of my table. Then go out and explain it as best you can to Caleb."

Caleb frowned as he listened to Richard's halting explanation. "Miz Bristol will be mighty mad, but she's already mad at your uncle. I'm sorry about the music lessons and

I'll miss hearing you play. Did your uncle say you can't talk to me?"

"No. He didn't say that."

Caleb grinned and punched Richard on the shoulder. "So we'll go right on being friends. We'll talk before school and after school. It won't matter a whole lot."

But it did. It mattered a lot to Richard.

CHAPTER
11

Although the snow was deep on the ground, there were wagon tracks to follow, and Richard never missed a day of school. On the fourth day of February more snow fell. By early afternoon the sky was dark and the wind had picked up and was howling around the little schoolhouse.

A farmer came with his wagon to pick up his children and other children who lived along the road to his house.

"The rest of you had better go home, too, if you live near," Mr. Dewey said. He checked with each child. Two said they would go to their grandmother's house in town. Others who lived a distance would go home with their friends.

"Miz Bristol is expecting Richard," Caleb said.

Mr. Dewey nodded in agreement, but Richard knew that he could not go to Mrs. Bristol's house. He pulled his stockings up over his pants legs. He wrapped his wool scarf around his nose and mouth and pulled his cap down over his forehead.

"You look like you were heading for the north country instead of Miz Bristol's," Caleb laughed.

Richard ran to the door and out to the road.

"Come back," Caleb called. "Miz Bristol wants you at her house."

"Have to get home," Richard called back over his shoulder without slowing.

Caleb continued to shout warnings, but Richard ignored him. He ran until his sides began to ache and he had to slow to a walk. Although the wind swirled the snow, the tracks in the road were visible and he strode along at a steady pace for several miles.

The sky grew darker. The wind picked up snow from the road and hurled it around his feet and into his boots. The cold bit right through his scarf and up his sleeves. The tracks in the road disappeared and for a moment he felt panic—until he saw a trace of the tracks ahead. The wind continued to erase the tracks, like an eraser on a slate.

When the tracks had completely disappeared, Richard watched the gray leafless trees marching along on either side of the road and tried to stay in the middle of the open space between them. And then the trees disappeared. He took a step and his foot went down and down. He fell into the ditch at the side of the road, but he got up and groped his way back up to the road.

He walked on. Then he was no longer following the road. He didn't know where he was. He didn't even know if he was going in the right direction. His toes and fingers were numb. He had no idea how long he had been on the road. He walked right into a tree, and felt blood trickle down his forehead and then freeze. His legs were heavy, his body ached. All he wanted to do was to sit down and rest, just rest. . . .

He remembered stories he had heard of men lost in storms in Vermont. He must not sit down; he would freeze to death in a very short time. He staggered on into the swirling dark curtain.

He collided with something knee high and fell head-first into a bank of snow. His body was too numb to be hurt. He brushed the snow off his face and tightened his scarf. The thing he had fallen over was a stone wall. If he followed the wall . . . Branches reached out and grabbed his cap. Where was it? He groped with his hands, as blind now as Granny Gates. When, at last, he had found his cap, he sat down on the wall.

He would never find his way in this storm and by morning he would be frozen to death. He pulled his recorder out of his back pocket and began to blow into it. He couldn't play a tune because his fingers were numb, so he just blew one loud note, the same note over and over. Someone might hear it—if Uncle Lyman and the boys were out looking for him and if they could hear anything over the howl of the wind.

He didn't know how long he had sat tooting when suddenly he heard a husky voice calling his name.

He jumped to his feet. "Here I am! Here!" He fought through a tangle of branches and ran toward the voice.

He banged into a hard body and was lifted up and swung over a shoulder like a bag of flour. Maybe he fainted; maybe he slept. . . .

He was on his feet just inside the barn, beside Boy, who was holding his sides and gasping for breath. Snow lay heaped on one shoulder of Boy's coat. Richard looked down and saw a puddle made from the snow that was melting from their boots.

"Thank you for finding me." Richard could hear a sob in his own voice. "Thank you."

Boy said nothing but turned toward the barn door.

"Hold on a minute there, Black Boy. Where you been?" Uncle Lyman swung the Negro around to face him. Uncle Lyman had not been out in the storm; his clothes were dry; so were Dan's and Zeke's.

"I was lost, Uncle Lyman," Richard said. "The wind erased the tracks in the road and then I couldn't even see the trees. I'd given up." Richard blinked back tears as he recalled his misery. "And there he was and he carried me all the way home."

"Where did you find him?" Uncle Lyman demanded.

Boy nodded off toward the road.

"Were you off my land?"

Boy nodded again.

"You know the penalty for leaving this land?"

Boy lowered his eyes.

Richard didn't know the penalty, but he knew that Uncle Lyman was very angry with Boy. "He was looking for me. He found me. I'd have died if he hadn't found me."

Uncle Lyman glanced at Richard. "Not likely," he said,

and then turned back to Boy. "How'd you know that Dick had gotten himself lost? Tell me, Boy."

Boy turned toward the door. Uncle Lyman picked up a whip and flicked it. "Tell me, Boy. How'd you know?"

Boy said nothing.

"Answer me, Boy."

Still the black man remained mute.

"Bare your back, Boy. Right now."

When Boy had removed his jacket and shirt, Uncle Lyman raised his long whip and hurled it down across Boy's back. It left a deep gash in the dark skin.

Richard leaped at his uncle and tried to wrest the whip from his hands. Dan pulled Richard away, threw him to the floor, and sat on him.

Uncle Lyman continued to whip his slave for what seemed like forever. Finally he stopped and threw the black man's shirt to him. Boy put it on over his bloody back. His big black fingers trembled.

The storm lasted for three days. Richard went to the lean-to to tell Boy how sorry he was, but the shutters were down over Boy's eyes. "You teach her to read," he said, and turned away.

"How'd you manage to get yourself lost, Dick?" Dan asked over and over. "Can't you even find your way home from school, Dick? What good's that book learnin' doin' ya?"

Richard hated his cousin Dan. He hated Uncle Lyman even more. *He killed Runt. I hate him for that and for taking me away from Bennington and telling me I can't sit with Caleb or play the pianoforte. Most of all, I hate him because he owns slaves and because he sold Dina away from her family and whipped Boy.*

Richard was so angry that it pained him to eat Uncle Lyman's food and sleep under Uncle Lyman's roof. He felt as if he were being ground into the earth under the heel of Uncle Lyman's boot. Only one thing eased his pain: planning his escape. Granny Gates and Georgina would miss him; Uncle Lyman would not. He hadn't cared enough about his "useless" nephew to look for him during the storm.

The pity was that Boy was so useful in the fields and Georgina was so useful in the house. If they were to run away, Uncle Lyman would search the world for them. Once he found them, he'd lock them up or put them in chains.

Could they escape if they were less useful? The answer was no. If Boy were found sleeping in the field or if he dropped a rock, he'd be beaten. Would Uncle Lyman beat Georgina if she spilled the milk or burned the mush? Richard didn't know, but he did know that Uncle Lyman would never let his slaves leave the farm.

How did Black Boy know I was lost? Richard asked himself that question over and over. Finally, when the road was passable and he could return to school, Caleb answered the question.

"When I got home I told my pa about this dumb friend of mine who thought he could walk five miles in a blizzard." Caleb punched Richard on the shoulder and grinned. "My pa and I went out on our old mule looking for you. Got all the way to Peck's place, but we didn't see you. So we told Boy, and the three of us spread out and headed across the fields toward town. Boy had a lantern and when he found you he waved it so we knew you were found and we went home."

"Thank you, Caleb." Richard wanted to hug his friend; he punched his shoulder instead.

"Weren't nothing, Richard. Just a blizzard. Ma said we looked like white rabbits when we got home. How's Boy? Bet he looked like the biggest white rabbit in the world."

"I don't know where I was when he found me but he carried me, slung over his shoulder. Must have been a long way because Boy was gasping for breath when we got to the barn. But he was all right until . . ." Richard bit his lip and turned away.

"Until what?"

"Until Uncle Lyman whipped him," Richard whispered, and ran into the schoolhouse.

Caleb ran after him. "Weren't your fault, Richard."

"I'm the one who got lost. If I'd stayed at Mrs. Bristol's, I might have been whipped, not Boy." There, he'd said it. Knowing that Boy had been whipped because Richard had made a bad decision was an additional burden. Richard owed his life to Boy.

CHAPTER
12

One noon hour when he was studying Greek with Mr. Dewey, Richard asked a question that had been bothering him: "How can slavery be allowed in New York when it is prohibited in Vermont?"

Mr. Dewey said that each state made its own laws about slavery. Since the revolutionary war most of the northern states, including Massachusetts and Connecticut, had abolished slavery. In New York a law had been passed that would end slavery eventually. Every baby born to a slave in New York since 1799 would become free, girls at the age of twenty-five and boys at the age of twenty-eight.

"Georgina was born before 1799. Why should she be a slave for the rest of her life? Her father, too. That's not fair."

"Many people agree with you, Richard. I'm hoping the law will be changed to free all slaves—maybe within a decade. In the meantime, it is illegal to export slaves out of New York or to import them into New York."

"So Uncle Lyman broke the law when he sold Georgina's mother and sent her south. Why didn't someone stop him?"

"I've been asking about that. Your uncle says he didn't sell her. He says he sent her to Pennsylvania for a short time. He makes it sound like a pleasure trip."

"It wasn't *her* pleasure. It took three men to drag her away from the door she was clinging to. That's what Georgina says. They put a chain on her ankle. She didn't want to go."

"She was with child. If her baby had been born in New York, it would be free in twenty-five years or twenty-eight years, and probably much sooner. If Girl's child lived, it has surely been sold in the South, and frankly, Richard, I suspect that Girl has been sold, too."

"So why doesn't somebody do something?"

"Because no one is sure what has happened and because your uncle is highly respected. He's a good farmer, generous with his neighbors, honest in his business dealings."

"And he bought slaves!"

"He didn't actually buy Girl. She was born to one of his father's slaves. He inherited her. He says that he bought Black Boy from a neighboring farmer to please Girl."

"But he sent her away from Boy and Georgina. Does that sound like he wanted to make her happy? I wonder where she is now."

"I'm trying to find out," Mr. Dewey said softly.

"You are?" Richard would have shouted if he dared.

"She and seven other slaves from the area went with a

Mr. Bridgewater, who took them west by wagon to the Susquehanna River, where he loaded them onto a flat-bottomed barge. I haven't heard anything about them after that, but I suspect they floated all the way down the Susquehanna to the Chesapeake Bay." Mr. Dewey traced the river on a large map. "I hear that the Susquehanna is too shallow for regular boats. As you see, it runs right through Pennsylvania. Many Quakers live there, and they're fighting slavery on every front. . . ."

"So maybe she escaped! A Quaker could have helped her. Maybe she's free and waiting for her family to join her." Richard's voice rose with excitement.

"Hush. We have no reason to believe that she has escaped. If she has, she would surely have found some way to contact her family by now. I hear that she's a spirited one." Mr. Dewey sat back in his chair and studied Richard's face. "I don't need to tell you that we must not discuss this with anyone, not even with each other. Should I hear more about Girl . . ."

"Her name is Dina."

"Should I hear more about Dina, I will let you know." He sighed. "Tell me about the slave child, Richard. What does she have to read? Is she making progress?"

"Oh yes. Georgina is smart. I loaned her my copy of *Puss in Boots*. The first couple of weeks she wrote words she didn't know in the dirt or in flour or ashes, whatever was handy when we were alone. I'd tell her the word, and she'd remember. She hasn't asked for my help for a long time. I'm sure she knows every word in the book."

Mr. Dewey nodded and then went to a shelf and

removed a tattered copy of the *New England Primer*. "Take this to her. Some of the pages are missing, but it will be something new to read."

The schoolmaster's gift delighted the child. "Tell that Mr. Dewey that Georgina, she be mighty pleased to read his nice book. You tell him that, Richard. You is a good boy to teach me to read and bring me books. I give your *Puss in Boots* book back now."

"Keep it, Georgina, if it gives you pleasure."

"It do. I keep it just a little longer."

And then it was sugaring time. Richard missed a week of school. He and his uncle and cousins were out every day tapping the maple trees. It was perfect sugaring weather, freezing nights and sunny days.

While they were tapping the trees, Boy was gathering wood for three fires and setting up frames to hold a huge pot over each fire. When the sap was emptied into the pots the fires had to be kept going constantly. The syrup had to be stirred from time to time. Uncle Lyman and Dan stayed up for the first half of the night, then they woke Zeke and Richard to tend the sugar during the second half of the night.

It was more entertainment than work because neighbors visited one another during the day to see who had the most sugar and the clearest syrup. One neighbor had a copy of the *Connecticut Courant* with news from the new capital in Washington. The House of Representatives had finally chosen Thomas Jefferson to be the president over Aaron Burr, who had received the same number of electoral votes. Burr was from New York so many of the neighbors had hoped he would win. Others favored Jefferson, who had written the Declaration of Independence. Discussions were lively. Richard was sorry when the sugaring was done.

"You did good work, Dick," Uncle Lyman said as they were dousing the fires. He handed him a loaf of sugar. "This is for you. You can take it to town and sell it for whatever you can get. Your money." He handed him another loaf. "And on your way to school Monday, take this to Granny's friend. Tell her we made too much and she'd be doing me a favor if she took this off my hands. Old Anna's proud; doesn't like to take from nobody."

Richard saw that his uncle also gave a very large loaf of sugar to Boy and another small one to Georgina. It would be easier, Richard thought, if Uncle Lyman never did anything nice. Then he could just plain hate him. But Uncle Lyman was not an all-bad man. *He* thought that he took good care of his slaves and of his clumsy nephew. He worked harder than anyone else on the farm. *He* thought that Runt had to be killed for food.

On a sunny day in the middle of April, when all of the other children were eating their lunches outside, Mr. Dewey and Richard remained indoors. They spread their lunches on the table in front of them.

"Eat and listen carefully to what I have to say," Mr. Dewey said in a low voice. "No one must hear me or even suspect that we are discussing anything other than the Greek language. Do you understand?"

107

Richard nodded.

"Since our last conversation about Georgina's family, I have sought out several whom I know to be sympathetic to the plight of slaves in this area. It seems that Dina did try to pass a message along to Black Boy, but the last person to receive it lives in Spencertown. He did not know whom to trust with the message. I told him he could trust you and me."

"He sure can. I'll get the message to Boy tonight." Richard jumped up and thrust out his hand to receive the paper.

Mr. Dewey put his finger across his lips and motioned for Richard to sit. "It is a word-of-mouth message. I will not deliver it to you unless you can assure me that you will be very careful, that you will not shout, and that you will deliver it to no one except Boy."

"You can"—his voice was loud; he lowered it to a whisper—"trust me."

"Fine. This is the message: Dina and the woman to whom she was chained jumped into the Susquehanna River in the night when everyone was asleep. They must have chosen a spot where the river was shallow so they could wade to the shore. They had the luck to meet up with a Quaker almost immediately. She hid them, and then she and other Quakers helped them escape to Canada. Dina is working as a cook in a boarding school in a small town just south of Montreal. She has the baby with her. A boy."

Richard wanted to jump up and dance and sing and shout with joy. Georgina's mother was safe! He clasped his hands in front of him to keep them still. He bit his lip. And then he said, very quietly, "I will deliver the message, sir."

"If Boy should wish to join his wife, I will help him."

"I'll help, too." Richard tried not to grin. He was supposed to be studying Greek—which was solemn work.

By the time Richard reached home that evening, he had concocted a plan to deliver the message to Boy and Georgina in their lean-to. After supper, Richard filled a tankard with water and drank it straight down. He refilled the tankard and sipped it while he read a chapter in *The Vicar of Wakefield*. Then he drank another tankard of water.

"You seem mighty thirsty tonight," Aunt Prudence said.

"Planning on spending the night in the privy?" Dan asked.

Exactly, Richard said to himself. "I don't know why I'm so thirsty. Must be the warm weather coming on."

Of course he would have to get up in the night; no one would think anything of it.

When everyone seemed to be asleep, he crept down the stairs, lit a lantern, and went out to the privy. Then, shading the lantern with his body, he slipped into the lean-to. Georgina was sleeping on a straw mattress near the door. He shook her.

"Don't say a word," he whispered. "Come over by your father." When he shook Boy, the man jumped up with a start. "Sit down. It's me, Richard. Come closer, Georgina. Don't make a sound but listen carefully. I have good news. Dina escaped. She is in Canada working as a cook in a school. The baby is a boy. He's with her."

"A brother?" Georgina whispered.

Boy pushed Richard and the straw mattress aside and began to dig in the dirt. Bewildered, Richard watched as Boy uncovered a rag pouch.

"Sugar money. He thinks I eat all that sugar, but Jacob sells it for me." Boy began to bundle his few clothes and blankets together. "Get ready," he said to Georgina. "We're travelin' on to Canada, tonight." Then he turned to Richard. "Which way is Canada?" he asked.

Richard had not imagined that Boy would think of setting out right away. He had been confined to this land for many years. "You couldn't get out of town without help." Richard sighed.

"They catch us, Mr. Lyman put us in chains," Georgina whispered. "We never see Mama."

Boy sat down with a thud.

"For tonight it is enough that you know that your wife and child are safe," Richard said. He rose and blew out the lantern. "You have friends who will help you. We'll make a plan. Just go on like nothing has happened. I will let you know."

Richard slipped across the yard and up the stairs.

"Told ya ya shouldn't drink so much water," Dan muttered as Richard climbed back into bed.

CHAPTER
13

During the Greek lesson the next noon, Richard reported to Mr. Dewey. "Boy was ready to run out into the night even though he didn't know which direction is north. I told him we'd come up with a safe plan. If only he knew the roads around here. He doesn't know how to get beyond Caleb's house. I suppose they'll have to go at night, on foot. They'll have to find places to hide during the day. Or maybe I could steal a wagon from Uncle Lyman, but where could I take them? If they don't make it the first time, it will be twenty times as hard a second time, because Uncle Lyman will lock them in at night and guard them during the day."

"So we'll have to do it right the first time. Tell Boy that his friends are making plans. Beg him to be patient."

That night when he had finished reading, Richard went to the privy and then slipped into the slaves' lean-to to deliver the message about patience.

"One thing I learned all these years is how to wait,"

Boy said sadly. "But it be hard when Dina and li'l George is waiting."

"George?" Richard asked.

"She name him George, like George Washington. Him a fine man. Ride a big white horse."

Richard was leaving the lean-to when Georgina touched his arm. When he turned toward her, she put the *Puss in Boots* book in his hand.

"You keep it," he said.

She shook her head.

He shoved the book toward her, but she turned her back. At last he shrugged and climbed back to the loft and put the book in his box.

After supper one evening, Uncle Lyman handed Richard a letter. "Seems old Ambrose hasn't forgotten you after all."

"You got a letter, Richard?" Granny Gates cackled. "Read it to us."

Richard bit his lip; he didn't want to read the letter aloud until he knew what was in it. Finally, he said just that.

To Richard's surprise, Uncle Lyman nodded his agreement. Richard excused himself from the table and took his letter to the fireplace. It was a short letter:

Dear Richard,

You will wonder why I have not written to you. When I received your letter I decided that you would be happier if you could think less about your life with Aunt Ruth and me here in Bennington. You have a new life now.

Business has been good. At first I was very lonely, missing you and Ruth. Last month, however, I married again. Faith is a fine young woman from Williamstown, Massachusetts. We will both welcome you, whenever you can visit us.

Your loving uncle

"Uncle Ambrose married a lady named Faith from Williamstown, Massachusetts," Richard said to the family.

"Didn't waste no time grieving for Ruth, did he?" Granny Gates muttered.

"Waited a year," Aunt Prudence said.

It was hard for him to believe that Uncle Ambrose could marry anyone. He had loved Aunt Ruth. How could he love another lady? He had said Richard was his son. Had he forgotten that, too?

Richard folded the letter and put it in his pocket. Georgina could use the blank spaces on the paper to practice writing.

The next week during a Greek lesson, Mr. Dewey discussed the slaves again. "I've been told of about a half dozen other slaves from nearby towns who may also want to go to Canada, so I've made this plan: When the school year ends, I'll leave town—for good. On the set day, I'll be waiting with a hay wagon at the grape arbor at a farm just over the border in Massachusetts. The owners of the farm are friends who want to help. I'll take the slaves straight through to Canada, stopping only to change horses along the way. Others will help the other slaves get to the grape arbor. Boy and Georgina will be our responsibility."

"I could take them. Leave when everyone was asleep."

"You'd have to stay off the roads. How are you going to find your way through the fields and woods in the night? A lantern could be seen. If only there were a day when everyone is busy inside. I've thought of Sunday during the service, but anyone who led the slaves would be missed at church and immediately associated with the crime. It is a crime, you know. Stealing a man's slaves is the same as stealing his money. You must consider that, Richard, before you become more deeply involved."

Richard had thought of what a grand thing he would be doing for Georgina and Boy. He would be a hero, though few would know of his fine deed. He hadn't thought of jail or, worse, the gallows. He rubbed his neck, imagining the cut of the rope.

And then an idea flashed into his head. "Fourth of July," he almost shouted. "Everyone in town will be at Mrs. Bristol's from morning until late afternoon."

"But you would be missed. I've heard how you played your recorder and then the pianoforte last Fourth of July. They will expect you to do it again."

"I could be sick," Richard suggested.

"If you were very sick, your aunt would stay home with you. If you were slightly sick, your uncle would know exactly whom to suspect when he came home to find his slaves gone. Besides, I doubt that you know the country-side around here well enough to lead them."

"I know Uncle Lyman's farm and the road to town. That's about it. But if I had a map I could follow it."

Mr. Dewey shook his head slowly from side to side while he continued to think. "We're going to have to bring in someone else. Jacob is the obvious person, but he's the first person your uncle would suspect."

Richard said one name over and over in his mind and then he whispered it: "Caleb. No one except Caleb's mother would know if he were gone for several hours."

"And you could make sure that he had all the time he needed. You could play your recorder and the pianoforte. You could get people to sing or to dance. You could do whatever is necessary to keep your uncle at Bristol's until Caleb returned after delivering Boy and Georgina."

"Where they will be free and safe in Massachusetts."

"Not free, Richard, and not safe. They won't be safe until they get to Canada. They are your uncle's property. If he finds them, he can bring them home, in chains if necessary."

Richard made one more nighttime trip to the lean-to to share the plan with Georgina and Boy and to tell them that it would be many days, almost two months, before they could leave.

During the last weeks of the school year, Richard concentrated on learning Greek. He went over letters and words in his brain as he walked to school every morning. Except on days when it rained, he played his recorder on the return trip. He didn't usually think about Runt until he was almost home.

"We're breaking our backs getting fields ready to plant while you just stroll along playing your tooter," Uncle Lyman complained one evening as Richard came into the barnyard. "Tell Mr. Dewey that he can forget planting ideas; we need you here to plant seeds."

"Friday's the last day of school." Richard laughed and then turned sad. "Mr. Dewey will be leaving on Saturday and he won't be back next year. Doubt I'll ever see him again."

"That won't grieve me none, Dick."

May and June of 1801 were just like the previous year. They worked from dawn to dusk planting. Boy, his eyes still shuttered, did the work of an ox. Richard picked rocks and planted corn and stole minutes to continue to teach Georgina to read.

"Your work is better this year," Uncle Lyman said one morning as they walked to the field. "Think you can plow straight?"

Careful, Richard warned himself. If he became a good worker, Uncle Lyman might come to value him. On the day that I run away, I want Uncle Lyman to say, "Good riddance." I do not want him to come looking for me. Richard grabbed the handles of the plow, but he did not hold it steady as the ox pulled it across the field. At the far edge, Richard turned the plow around and the ox pulled it back to where Uncle Lyman stood scowling at the wavy furrows.

"A drunk could plow straighter rows than you can, Dick," he snarled, pushing the boy aside and calling to Dan.

"Guess I'd better go back to picking rocks," Richard said.

"Best thing for Dick," Zeke called. When Uncle Lyman turned away, Zeke grinned at his cousin.

Does Zeke know that I could be a better farmhand? Does he know why I'm not? Richard dropped fewer rocks and hoed more carefully, but he made sure that planting corn was the only task he did better than Dan.

CHAPTER
14

On the night of July third, Richard kept his eyes closed and lay perfectly still, pretending to sleep. Dan must not know that he was awake. Tomorrow night when Uncle Lyman discovered that his slaves had escaped he would ask everyone about everything. If Dan were to say, "Dick here couldn't sleep last night," Uncle Lyman would say, "Why was that, Dick? You never had trouble before. What do you know about Gee Gee and Boy?" That was a question Richard hoped never to be asked.

In the morning he lingered in the loft until everyone was downstairs. Then he took the *Puss in Boots* book from his box and stuffed it in his shirt. The cows had been milked and Richard drove them to the pasture. He slipped into the lean-to on his way to breakfast, took the book from his shirt, and opened the book so that she would see this message as soon as she picked up the blanket she would be taking with her: To Georgina from her friend Richard Baldwin, Independence Day, 1801.

When the animals had been fed, Boy hitched the pair

of horses to the wagon and Georgina helped load the pot of baked beans and the pies and the cakes. Uncle Lyman and Aunt Prudence and Granny Gates shared the wagon seat. The boys, holding their bucket drums, sat with their legs dangling from the back of the wagon.

As the horses stepped out toward the lane, Richard waved one finger at Georgina. Standing in front of the door in her too-big dress, she looked straight at him, neither smiling or speaking. They dared not say good-bye.

For a moment, Richard was sad. His life seemed to be just one good-bye after another. He would miss the little girl. But how can I be sad? he asked himself. Boy and Georgina are heading toward freedom with Dina and the baby. Families are supposed to be together. His sadness flew away, but anxiety settled in his stomach like a great rock. What if something goes wrong? Earlier he had been so frightened that he'd had to force himself to eat breakfast.

"Never knew your appetite to leave you, Dick," Uncle Lyman had boomed. Everyone at the breakfast table had turned to look at his plate.

Think quickly, Richard had commanded himself. "I'd thought to save space for all the treats at the celebration, but I guess I'm just too hungry. It's not in my nature to put off eating." He had laughed and lifted a huge spoonful of mush to his lips.

Georgina and Boy will have just this one chance. If they are returned to Uncle Lyman after trying to escape, he will surely keep them locked up—if he doesn't sell them in the South, farther away from Dina and away from friends like Caleb who want to help them. They must not fail this chance. Richard wondered if anyone could see his heart beating against his shirt.

The parade to Bristol's was better than last year. They had one real drum and more children with lids. Richard played "Yankee Doodle" with lots of trills and additions of his own devising. His fingers and his mouth made music while his mind was back at the farm.

Georgina was supposed to finish up the dishes and straighten the kitchen and bank the fire. Boy was supposed to clean the stalls. That would take about half an hour. In half an hour the wagon would be at Bristol's and the horses would be unhitched and herded into an enclosure.

Then Georgina and her father were to put on their shoes and pick up the two bundles they had prepared. They would walk to the grove of maples in the northeast corner of Uncle Lyman's property. Caleb would meet them there. Caleb's father had gone with him over the route they would take.

As the troop of children marched into Mrs. Bristol's yard, Caleb let out a whoop. "I wanted to be in the parade," he shouted. That was part of the plan; everyone must take notice of Caleb. When they didn't see him again, they'd just think that he was someplace else, if they thought about him at all.

The same old man read the Declaration of Independence, but he read it even more slowly, which pleased Richard, who wanted everything to go slowly. By the time the reading was finished, Caleb would be nearing the place he was to meet Boy and Georgina.

The minister prayed. Richard prayed, too, silently. He thanked God for a perfect day, hot but with a breeze. It was a good day for travel and a good day to spend in Mrs. Bristol's yard with neighbors.

Please, God, take care of Boy and Georgina and Caleb and Mr. Dewey. He said the line over and over. He didn't want to take God's attention away from his friends today. Later he would ask God to help him escape, too.

Although Richard was not hungry, he took enough food so that no one would notice his lack of appetite. He climbed under the branches of a huge weeping willow tree and forced himself to eat. Back at the food table he said that Caleb had asked him to get him another piece of turkey. He spoke loudly so that many people would hear him and believe that Caleb was near at hand. When he had eaten the turkey he said was for Caleb, he climbed out from under the willow and sat on a log until Zeke and Caroline came looking for him.

"Where ya been?" Zeke asked. "We wanted you to play us a tune, Dick."

"Caleb and I ate our dinners under that big old weeping willow."

"Hiding, eh? So Pa wouldn't see you with Caleb. Where's he now?"

"Helping his ma in the kitchen," Richard lied. "What do you want me to play, Miss Caroline?"

While Richard played for Zeke and Caroline, little children began a noisy game of tag. Dan and his friends turned cartwheels and walked the fence. The girls their age stood around and tittered. Many of the men went out to the horse enclosure to discuss possible trades and sales. The women gathered together the eating utensils they had brought with them, and began to assemble chairs and benches in the shade near where Richard was playing. The longer he played, the more people came to listen and then to sing along. A few young people danced on the lawn.

Eventually Richard ran out of tunes to play. He played many of them a second time. Then he encouraged everyone to sing without accompaniment. Several young girls sang solos.

"Why don't you come inside and play a piece on the pianoforte for us, Richard?" Mrs. Bristol said. "Caleb can also play."

Richard jumped to his feet and headed toward the house. He smiled with his lips while inwardly he groaned. They had decided not to tell Mrs. Bristol of their plans because Richard and Mr. Dewey wanted her to be able to say, truthfully, that she knew nothing about Uncle Lyman's slaves.

"Where is Caleb?" Mrs. Bristol asked. "I haven't seen him since . . ."

"He's around. We ate together. . . ." Richard tried to look as if he expected to see Caleb behind a tree.

"Oh that boy!" Mary stood on the doorstep with her hands on her hips. "He ate till he was sick, silly boy. I had to send him home to lie down."

Richard's eyes met Caleb's mother's eyes and held for a second. Mary was a good liar. Then he ran on inside and played every piece he knew. The women, and most of the men, gathered near the open windows.

"Enough of that, Dick," Uncle Lyman called. "Time to head for home."

"Oh, Lyman, that boy is giving us such a treat," one old lady said.

"Let him play a little longer," said another.

Richard played a hymn. He looked toward the door. Mary was standing there. She shook her head slightly. Caleb had not yet returned. So far Richard's job, keeping everyone entertained at the Bristol farm, had been easy. Now is the time for me to be clever, he said to himself.

"More food?" Mary suggested.

"Oh, yes. Do come back to the table. There is so much. . . ." Mrs. Bristol begged her guests to follow her to the table.

"I'm stuffed like a Christmas goose," one man said.

"Couldn't eat another bite," said a woman.

"Good idea," said Richard, jumping up from the piano and heading for the door, hoping that he'd see Caleb loping through the fields toward the house.

Caleb was not in sight. The trip was supposed to take about four hours, maybe five. He should have been back—unless something had gone wrong. Had he lost the way?

"Nothing more for us," Uncle Lyman shouted. "Come on boys, Granny."

Think of something. The rock in Richard's stomach was a boulder. His breath came in gasps. He had to do something to keep Uncle Lyman at Mrs. Bristol's until Caleb returned. If Uncle Ugly were to discover that his slaves were missing and that Caleb was missing, too, the whole plan would fail. The slaves might be captured. He couldn't imagine what Uncle Lyman would do to Caleb and perhaps to other members of Caleb's family, but he knew that it would be violent. *The safety of many is in my hands.*

Dan and four of his friends were walking toward him. Richard swallowed and stepped forward. He stuck out his foot so that the boy named Tom tripped and fell to the ground. Several people laughed. Tom jumped to his feet, his face red, his pale eyes glaring.

"Last year you said I was a sissy. You want to fight about it?" Richard raised his fists.

Tom swung wildly and Richard stepped aside. More people laughed. Tom's face turned purple. He lifted his right fist. Richard ducked to the left. Tom's left fist slammed into Richard's stomach. He gasped and staggered. He must not fall. *Where are you, Caleb?* He charged at Tom with his head. Tom stepped back and swung his fist into Richard's jaw; his teeth rattled. Tom hit again; his nose began to bleed.

"Get him, Tom!" Dan shouted.

"Get the sissy, get the sissy!" the boys chanted together. "Get him, get him, get him, Tom!"

Richard made a fist and swung blindly. His fist crashed into the side of Tom's face. He hit him again.

"Fight, Dick, fight!" Zeke shouted.

"Stop!" shouted Caroline and some of the girls. "You're hurting each other!"

Tom swung back and hit Richard in the stomach.

Richard fell. Tom fell on top of him and began hitting his face. Richard grabbed Tom's shoulders and pushed. The boys rolled together in the grass and once again Richard was on his back and Tom was sitting on top of him. Tom socked him in the eye. Such pain!

Richard's will to fight oozed out of his body. I'm sorry, Caleb, he cried to himself as tears stung his eyes. He dropped his hands from Tom's shoulders and turned his head to one side. It took all the strength left in his body to keep tears from seeping beneath his eyelids.

And then he heard sounds more beautiful than the organ music he had heard in Boston. Caleb was running through the Bristol yard, shouting. "Hey there, Tom! You lay off my friend. Want to fight more, you can fight me." He pushed Tom off of Richard and held out his hand to help Richard stand up. He grinned and tilted his head forward an inch or two. All is well, he was saying without words. I delivered Georgina and Boy to Mr. Dewey. They are on their way to Canada. Our plan worked.

Richard returned the grin and the nod, though the tears were still floating in his eyes. One trickled down his sweaty cheek.

"Get away, you little darky." Uncle Lyman pushed Caleb aside and put his arm around Richard. "Not a bad fight for a beginner." He patted Richard's shoulder. "We'll get you home and take care of that eye, and your nose, and whatever other bruises you got." Uncle Lyman spoke loudly, calling everyone's attention to Richard's injuries as if they were medals of honor. "This boy—most of you know he's my own flesh and blood, the son of my dead sister—looked like a plucked goose when I brought him here little over a year ago. Look at him now. I'm makin' a real man of Dick."

Richard's nose was no longer bleeding when the horses turned into the farmyard, but his eye was swollen shut so that he could not see out of it. He was deciding that there was no spot on his body that did not hurt, when the wagon stopped. The cows were bawling.

"What the hell are them cows doing standing there at the barn door with full udders. Why haven't they been milked? Boy? Get out here, Boy, and explain yourself."

Out of his good eye, Richard saw Uncle Lyman stride off toward the lean-to. Zeke began to unhitch the horses. Dan ran to let the cows into the barn.

Aunt Prudence helped Granny Gates down from the wagon. "You come on inside, Richard," she called back over her shoulder.

"I better help Dan milk," he said.

Cows who are not milked on schedule are miserable. He felt responsible for their pain, so he went into the barn and lifted the clean pails from their nails and sat on the stool beside Bessie. His hands hurt so that he could hardly press Bessie's teats.

He thought about the events of the day. He had been so relieved when he had heard Caleb's voice. And then Uncle Lyman had started crowing about the fight. When the cow's udder was empty, Richard stood up and kicked the pail, spilling the milk on the barn floor.

"No sign of Boy!" Uncle Lyman shouted as he ran past the barn door toward the house. "Or of Gee Gee."

"Dick spilled a whole pail of milk," Dan said, following his father. "He sure is clumsy, ain't he, Pa? Couldn't even win a little old fight."

Uncle Lyman went into the house, where he paced back and forth from the fireplace to the window, swearing at Boy. "Probably fell asleep in the woods. Boy knows the boundaries. He wouldn't leave the land."

"Unless they ran away," Dan suggested cheerfully.

"Couldn't do that," Zeke drawled. "Boy don't even know the way to town. Maybe they're up at Jacob's place, having a little Independence Day celebration of their own."

"I'll whip him. I'll whip him good. Gee Gee, too." Uncle Lyman went to the door. "Saddle up, Zeke," he commanded. "Dan, you strain the milk. Ask Prudence to tend to them bruises, Dick."

Richard woke very early the next morning and lay thinking about the day before. He pictured the wagon rolling along through Vermont toward Canada. "Thank you, God," he whispered to himself.

When he could lie still no longer, he sat up, painfully, and looked across Dan's sleeping body to the empty side of the bed. Zeke was not there. He stumbled on the stairs and realized that he could only see out of one eye. The other was still swollen shut. He touched his cheek, which was tender.

He left the privy door open so that there would be light to look at his body. He was black and blue—and green and yellow. He smiled. The fight hadn't been all that bad.

As he stepped out of the privy, the gander spread his wings and ran toward him.

"Get out of here, you nasty bird!" Richard shouted.

The gander folded his wings and turned away.

Dan and Richard had milked the cows and were eating breakfast when Uncle Lyman and Zeke rode into the yard.

Uncle Lyman entered the kitchen and dropped down at the end of the table. His shoulders sagged. His mustache drooped. His jaw was shaded. His eyes were lifeless.

"Did you go to Jacob's?" Aunt Prudence asked.

"Jacob and Mary and all the children were there. They were surprised when I told them that Boy and Gee Gee had disappeared. They said they hadn't seen them for months."

"You believe 'em, Pa?" asked Dan.

"Don't know. Miz Bristol says she doesn't know a thing either. Don't know if I can believe her either. Nasty woman. Said she *hoped* they had run away. We spent the night lookin'."

"Anyone help?"

"Paddy and Joe. Everyone else made excuses. Too much celebration. Too much work."

Zeke, looking almost as tired as his father, entered the kitchen. "Truth is, Ma, that folks around here don't have much interest in hunting runaway slaves."

"They're my property." Uncle Lyman banged the table with his fist. "And I treat 'em good."

Richard got up from the table and began to strain the milk. With his back to the rest of the family, he smiled.

Uncle Lyman and Zeke slept for a few hours and then set out for Massachusetts and Vermont. They returned three days later.

"No trace of them," Uncle Lyman said. "I can't think how they could have gotten away without help. Who would have helped them? Jacob? He was at Mrs. Bristol's all day. I saw him myself. Every soul from this town was there. One of Jacob's boys? I saw the older boys, too, and Zeke said that you had dinner with Caleb, Dick." Uncle Lyman scowled. "How many times do I have to tell you to stay away from that darky, Dick? I catch you with him again, I'll whip you. Hear me? I'll whip you."

"A slave from Chatham and two from Spencertown disappeared, too," Zeke said.

"Maybe we should have gone south to look for them, or over to the river. Maybe a thief visited all them darkies while we was celebrating. Told 'em he'd take 'em to the promised land. Could be they're all the way to the South by now. Gone for good." Uncle Lyman sighed sadly.

Then he changed the subject. "Saw your uncle Ambrose in Bennington, Dick. Him and his new wife. Nice-looking lady. She's going to give old Ambrose a child of his own. Hope it's a girl. He raises sissy boys. I told him so. And I told him I'm makin' a man of you, Dick. Told him you lost your fight but at least you went at it with spirit. I also told him that since you'd been doing real work you'd slimmed down and stretched up."

Uncle Lyman bought an ox and hired a young man to do the work Boy had done. He hired a young woman to help Aunt Prudence in the house and garden. She was older and larger than Georgina, but no stronger. The hired helpers were paid on Saturdays and went home to see their families on Sundays.

Richard did the same field work he had done the previous summer, picking rocks and hoeing and harvesting.

The work was easier because his body was stronger but he was not more skilled; he made sure of that.

One day Uncle Lyman asked him to mend a rock fence. Fitting the rocks together was like working out the fingering on a keyboard. He had to think ahead. If he put this rock here, would he have space for that rock there?

"Good work!" Uncle Lyman shouted when he examined the mended fence. Later he told Aunt Prudence that their nephew had the makings of a fine fence builder.

Richard didn't want to be a fine fence builder. Once again he had to stay awake until everyone was asleep so that he could go out and repair his stupid mistake. He removed rocks so that others fell on both sides of the fence.

"Guess I didn't do the foundation right," he whispered as Uncle Lyman stood staring at it the next morning. "I'm sorry."

But, of course, he wasn't really sorry.

One afternoon when Dan had scythed almost twice as much grain as his cousin, Uncle Lyman shook his head sadly. "Have you no pride, Dick?"

Richard hung his head. He spoke no words aloud but his inner voice, the voice that only he could hear, was clear: The truth is, Uncle Ugly, that I have a great deal of pride. I taught Georgina to read and I helped her and her father escape to Canada. I'm proud of that. True, I don't have much talent for farming, but I could learn to do most farm jobs if I had to. I was a leaf in a stream when I first came here from Bennington. No longer. I'm taking control of my life. That's my pride.

* * *

Sunday afternoons Richard crept away from the house to meet Caleb. Early in August Caleb brought a letter Mr. Dewey had written to him in Mrs. Bristol's care:

Dear Richard,

I have completed a journey which has been successful and ended happily for all. I am now back in Schenectady reading law with Judge Bates. I have recently talked with some interesting people. The master of a fine academy says that he will be needing someone to help with the fires and the garden. The job goes to a student. The organist at Saint George's Church says he will be needing a strong lad to pump the organ. I leave you with an old proverb: Where there is a will, there is a way. Please share my news with those who are interested.

Your friend,
Jonathan Dewey

Richard handed the letter to Caleb, who read it once and then again.

"This mean you'll be leaving?" Caleb asked.

Richard nodded. "I hadn't set a time. I thought maybe next year. But this letter changes things. If I could work and go to school and learn to play the organ all at the same time, wouldn't that be just the greatest thing?"

"What about your family here?"

"Uncle Lyman won't care when I leave. He values rough, nasty boys like Dan, not bumblers like me. Granny

Gates is the one who will miss me. The books and the music give her pleasure."

"Maybe Dan'll read to her."

Richard laughed. "Not him. Zeke maybe. Zeke doesn't say much, but I like him. I'm proud to be his cousin."

"I'll miss you, Richard." Caleb's raisin eyes looked sad as he punched Richard's shoulder. "But I'm willing to help you leave."

"You're a good friend, Caleb. Could you give Mr. Dewey's letter to Mrs. Bristol and ask her to let him know that I'm coming? I won't ask you to do anything else. I won't even tell you when I'm going." Suddenly an idea popped into his head. "But if anyone asks about me, you might just say that I often talked about Boston."

Caleb looked confused. "I heard you mention Boston just once, when you told me about the music at a church there." Then he grinned. "I see. Boston is in the opposite direction, isn't it? Write to me sometime, and I'll come to hear you play the organ—when I'm grown-up and you are, too."

That evening after supper, Richard turned to Granny Gates. "Did I ever tell you about the time I went to Boston?" he asked.

"You been to Boston, boy?" she cackled. "Tell us."

Richard did. He told everyone in the family about the wonders of the big city. "One day I want to go back there," he said.

"I been to Albany," Dan boasted. "Rode to the Hudson River and took a ferryboat 'cross it."

"A ferryboat? Weren't you scared, Dan? What if it turned over and sank? Can you swim, Dan?" Richard put fright into his eyes and voice. Inside he was laughing merrily, knowing that very soon he would make the trip to Albany and then on to Schenectady. "Me, I'd rather go to Boston. There are a couple of rivers to cross but none as wide and deep as the Hudson. I sure wouldn't want to cross the Hudson River."

That night, before he went to sleep, Richard made more plans. His body had grown strong; he could work all day in the fields and he could easily walk five miles to school and five miles home. He was glad of that. On a clear evening he'd drink a lot of water before he went to bed. That way he'd be sure to wake up in the middle of the night. His pack would be hidden in the fields. He'd pick it up and set out. He could walk in the middle of the road, unless he heard steps and had to hide.

He wouldn't go into the town because someone might be awake and looking out of a window. Instead, he would cut through Mrs. Bristol's farm to a road that led to the new turnpike. Later he might pick up a ride with a farmer or a peddler traveling from Massachusetts to the Hudson. He had the money from the sale of his maple sugar. If it was enough to pay for the ferry across the river, he could be in Albany by nightfall. Maybe he could help a storekeeper load shelves in exchange for a meal and a place to sleep. Then he'd ask for directions to Schenectady.

Before the end of the first week in September, Richard Baldwin planned to be in the town where he would learn to play the organ and where he would study Greek and read great books and learn complicated mathematics. His life would not be easy but it would be the life he chose. One day he might even come back to the farm—for a short visit.